NEVER GIVE UP

Never Give Up

Finding your fighting spirit

DAWN LA PUMA

The Serendipity Gallery

Publishing Details
Title: Never Give Up

First published 2021
Publisher: The Serendipity Gallery
Interior and Cover layout Pickawoowoo Publishing Group

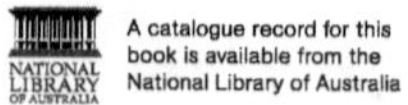

A catalogue record for this book is available from the National Library of Australia

ISBN 978-0-6450329-0-1 (paperback)
ISBN 978-0-6450329-1-8 (ebook)

Contents

Mum

I say to Mum 'I hate being small, I hate being picked
on by the bigger kids, why am I so small.'
Mum looks at me with affection in her eyes and a
smile on her face. She holds my face in her hands
and says: -
'God's not stupid!'

My Mum meant everything to me. Even now, years after her passing, I am filled with love and a deep sense of loss when I think of her. Love and pride for who she was and sadness as she is gone but also sad because her life was not what it should have been, and I couldn't fix that.

Mum came to Australia as an infant. She came by ship and it is amazing that she made it at all as in the ship's cabins babies were being attacked, by rats. An exhausted mother falling asleep to awake to her baby either dead or disfigured for life. Luckily Mum made it is one piece.

In my mind's eyes I see Mum standing on the porch of the old weatherboard house, watching us go off to school. She would stand there a while and then go indoors to continue the day's work. She would have started her day much earlier. There were a lot of us. I'm the 7th kid in a long line of kids 3 Boys and 3 girls before me then one girl and one boy after me, the boy was still born but I don't remember anything about it as I was too young to remember when he was born. Sam is also gone now. I was born on a cold winter night in June at the local hospital in Katanning, I was a big baby, nine pounds and seven ounces. Don't know what that is in kilograms but big I believe.

Mum was tall and she was a big woman, she wasn't fat but she wasn't skinny either. She was solid. Solid in every way. She was the prettiest woman I ever knew, now and then. She always wore a dress; one she had made herself, a pretty floral material was usually her choice. She would wear sensible shoes, shoes to walk in. She only ever wore dress shoes, as she called them, when she went dancing. Mum had lovely black hair and brown eyes, she rarely wore any makeup and I never saw her with lipstick on.

Mum was at ease with herself and she didn't mind walking around the house without her clothes. It seemed natural to us. I remember Mum had the bad habit of screwing up her face when she was thinking or concentrating on something or someone. I often hoped it wasn't something I had done, or not done.

I remember sneaking away when Mum and Dad would argue. This happened often as Dad would freak out over anything to do with money usually, but just about anything could set him off. There were a lot of us and the monthly food bill would be a constant threat to our peace. Dad would yell at Mum and she would end up in tears. He never physically struck her but I could see it hurt her having to go through this all the time. I felt powerless and frustrated with my own inadequacies to help her, to make him stop. What was wrong with him?

Dad would go out to the pub quite often and come back shouting and yelling about something that had pissed him off at some stage during the day. Sometimes us kids and Mum would wait for him in the car, outside the pub, for hours in the heat. He would bring her out a cold pub squash but never anything for us. Every now and then, when she had had enough, Mum would actually go in and pull him out, frog marching him to the door. There are some of my friends that say they remember, 'your Mum grabbing your Dad and pulling him out by the scruff of his neck'. She was brave.

One night when I was about twelve years old Dad went to the Pub, as he usually did. He was there a while, and when he came home he declared he was done with the pub and it had seen the last of him. He never did return to the pub for a drinking session. To this day there is no explanation as to this decision.

I always stuck up for Mum, her life was hard and I loved her. Dad wouldn't let her drive the car unless she was with him and she was not allowed to go anywhere without him or one of us kids. The kid that was accompanying her was almost always me as the others managed to find ways to get out of it. I felt sorry for her as she would not be able to go anywhere at all without one of us so I often gave up a night at the pictures with my friends or frogging or some such thing to a go with her. I mostly hated going to the dances as I was usually the only kid there and there was nothing for me to do.

Childhood

I think childhood was mostly fun except for all the shit that happened.

Mum is yelling at me, 'get inside and get to bed. Get out of the way before your Father gets here. Have you washed today? Boy you stink! Get a bath and go to bed'.

I sniff under my arm, Phew I am a bit wiffy but who cares and why should I get out of his way? Dad? Not really, not in any true sense of the word, all he thinks about is him. He is a big man in town. Everyone resects him and his Rotary and his Masons. Everyone gets his attention everyone except us. His family. That's how I see it.

I look across the room and roll my eyes at my Mum I know she wants to keep me out of trouble I know she wants to just get through the night and get to bed herself. I smile at my little baby brother Sam a couple of kids down from me and he's gorgeous. I love his big round face and his oval eyes. I hear the talk. There's something wrong with him. Well I don't see it. I see sweet and gentle and smiley. I see love. I love to cuddle him and I do now. He smells like a baby even though he's not, Mum spoils him with lots of attention. He has Down's Syndrome. Not sure what that is but I don't care, him and Mum are the only really good things in my life. The only two people that I love unconditionally.

I go into the old bathroom. Our house is not great but it's pretty good and it's on a farm, near a railway track, so it's a great place to live. The house is an old weatherboard and rammed earth home. There is a Metter's wood stove in the kitchen. A wooden table, with a piece of vinyl nailed to the top with wooden chairs squashed around it, is in the middle of the room. Nothing is new and shiny. The kitchen is tiny with whitewashed walls, as is most of the inside of the house. The doors have been stained brown with Condi's crystals and there is a timber floor. Outside there is a small creek running near the fence and attached to the house is a rainwater tank, our only water supply. We did not have electricity and we would use candles. Occasionally we used the generator but Dad did not consent to this luxury very often.

Later in my childhood the creek flooded and our little house was over taken by the rising water. The house was ruined and we all moved up to live in the shed until a new house was built. This one had electricity. We had a black and white TV then, an amazing luxury. Many years later, just a week after Dad passed away we got our first colour TV.

I remember as an adult going back to look at the old farm and finding part of the old mud house still standing. The Metter's stove was still there and inside cooking away over the years was a series of my best mud pies. I didn't disturb them. I climbed up to look in the water tank that was rusting away at the side of the ruins and found the skeleton of Mummy Cat. Mummy Cat, one of the much loved farm cats, had gone missing back in the days we were drinking that water. I don't think it hurt us but I can't be too sure. We were all horrified and tried to pretend it was a different cat but the evidence was too strong and we had to accept that we had not had the most sanitary upbringing in many ways.

I look at the water in the bath. A few kids have already been through and I add hot water to the already brown water. It's clay country here so we are always dirty and we really don't care. It's Mum who wants us clean. I get in and reluctantly pick up the old face washer and rub at the dirty parts. Under my arms, my crutch, around the back of my balls and then I wash my face and feet, then lastly I rub my neck. If I think about those days now I probably should have changed the order but who cares. I sniff under my arms again and it smells like soap so I know I'm good. I get out and get my pajamas on, say goodnight to Mum and fight my way through the other kids to get a cuddle of Sam, then I'm off to bed.

There's no such thing as privacy or peace and quiet at our place and that suits me fine. I'm not into reading and I don't want a place to do homework. I hate school and everyone there knows that I avoid it as often as I can. When I do go its usually to keep Mum quiet and so Dad doesn't get involved in the situation.

I love to play on the railway track and especially love to hear, and feel, the power of the fully laden trains as they thunder past, just a few meters from our gate. I don't say garden as we didn't have a garden. Mum didn't have time and Dad was useless. He was a farmer not a bloody gardener. A few odd geranium plants survived in pots on the long verandah but in truth it was an ugly yard in an ugly paddock. The only great and exciting thing about our place is the railway track.

I liked to put stones or rocks on the track to watch the trains crush them. I loved the explosion. Some of the rocks I dragged down there were as big as I could carry and I was pretty strong. One day officials from the railway came around to talk to Dad about the rocks on the track. The drivers were complaining and suggesting a possible derailment. My eyes lit up. WOW! Now that would be exciting for sure. But as usual my fun was curtailed. Dad shouted for me to, 'get over here now' I did and I was given a lengthy and impressive dressing-down. How did he know it was me? He just did. I did not stop but I chose smaller rocks. More because of Dad then any concern for the trains.

I would get as close to the trains as I could without being killed. I would even hide in the culverts under the track just to get the full experience. I dragged one of my little sisters in one day. I thought she would feel the same excitement as me but she was terrified and raced screaming to Mum as soon as the train had passed. No need to tell you what happened to me. I often got the strap. Mum would give it to us with a razor strop. I hated getting hit, and especially by Mum, but she was the one who metered out the discipline. Dad just yelled at us and called us idiots and stupid and in general made us feel bad.

The trains at this time were steam and this was very exciting. The trains were noisy and smoky and from time to time they belched hot coal. Occasionally these lumps of burning coal started fires along the track. In harvest season this was a bit of a worry. All the kids raced along the side of the tracks putting the fires out. Well, most of the kids I should say, I dragged sticks and branches to get a good fire going. Loved it all. I just sometimes got carried away with the excitement of life - the possibilities.

Talking about the trains reminds me of the old aboriginal couple that lived on our farm in a faded, white, old army issue, canvas tent, not far from the house. Winnie, worked as a nannie and she helped Mum. I remember as a little kid she would toss her naked breasts over her shoulder as she leaned to pick us up. Gradually they would come flopping back down to the front and I lived in terror of getting smothered by one of them. She was a delight though and loved us kids. Her hubby Elijah was a bit of a drinker and he would wander down to the pub around sunset and then later in the evening, when he was blotto, follow the tracks back to the farm. When the steam trains turned to diesel this proved fatal for Elijah. Dad warned him about the trains making no sound, but he didn't listen. One night one crept up on him not far from our house and Dad brought him out from under the train in two parts. I'll never forget this. I'm not sure what happened to Winnie after this. I can't remember, just those two things standout. The body under the train, split into two halves, and the boobs. Both equally terrifying.

There were around thirty Aboriginal people in the mob that lived on the farm. They had lived here for a long as I could remember and even before that. Mum said they had always been there. I was fascinated by these people and I was always down there playing with the kids. We all went to the same school, most of the kids were aboriginal. One of the boys gave me a bullroarer. A bullroarer is an Aboriginal musical instrument that was used in ceremonies and in hunting to flush out the prey. It was also used for communicating over long distances. He showed me how it worked. I loved that gift. I loved whirling it around and listening to the noise that it made. I was a child and I thought these people had the best of all lives. The innocence of childhood worked for all us kids. I was always with the kids, playing at home and at school, there were more Aboriginal kids at the school than white kids, back in those days.

One day I went with one of the Aboriginal kids from school to his house in town, he was my mate.

When I walked inside I was hit by the smell and I said to him, 'gees man, this place stinks'. A few days later he came for a sleep over and came inside, sniffed the air, and said, 'bloody stinks in here let's go outside'. To this day I don't know if it did stink to him or if he was playing me, anyway we both laughed and outside we went to discover what mischief we could get in together. Life appeared simple back then.

The Aboriginal people did a bit of work on the farm but mostly just went about their own business. My Dad tolerated them as long as they kept out of trouble and did not do anything that he would be upset with – they understood the rules. Dad would kill a sheep and take it to them every month or so. I'm not sure how this was paid for but knowing Dad it would definitely be paid for one way or another. Stealing was one of Dad's biggest hates and so it was a rule he upheld vigorously. So his reaction the day he found a little girl, of around nine years of age, picking grapes from our vines and popping them childishly into her mouth, was immediate and ruthless. He grabbed her by her arm and dragged her down to the camp. He shouted at the mob, who had all come running at the sound of the child's crying. He said everyone was to pack up and be off his land by nightfall or he would punish them all. The men begged him to reconsider telling him they would deal with the child and it would not happen again. Dad reluctantly agreed, reasserting vehemently that it was a final warning. The next morning the little girl had been severely beaten, she was covered in blood and bruised all over. I remember being horrified when I saw her. I also remember how many grapes we had, grapes that fell to the ground and went to rot. The Aboriginal families stayed with us for many more years and then one morning everyone had disappeared. No indication that they were going or where, no words spoken, just moved on, they had gone walkabout.

I learned a lot from the Aboriginal kids, one was how to use a bullroarer and scare the roos into the path of a shooter. They also taught me about bush tucker, and I was keen to try eating goanna. Eventually Dad caught one and we cooked it in the paddock to eat. I want to say it tasted like chicken but it didn't, it tasted like fish to me. In that same field one day a huge Race Horse goanna found itself exposed in open ground and sought somewhere to hide. Well Dad was the tallest tree in the paddock and the goanna raced up him and sat on his hat. Dad was panicked, jumping around on the spot and clawing at his head. It was one of the best moments of my childhood up to that point. Not a good moment for Dad though.

I was a skinny kid with long blonde hair, which was usually messy. I had very dark brown eyes and I always looked like I had just been into mischief or I was planning it. I usually was or had, so that fitted fine. I was a cute kid and Mum often told me my face would get me in trouble but I don't think it was my face that did that. I just had a knack for it. As a kid I was obsessed with how things worked and how they were made. I would go to great lengths to find out. One time I hammered out a penny. Got it as flat as I could, it was paper thin. Dad went mad. Not because he was worried about me but because he said I had wasted the money. The penny could not be spent in this flat condition. That was my Dad for you. Poor Mum she was constantly patching me up and keeping me out of more trouble.

Once I managed to break the surface of a golf ball. I began to peel and unwind the rubber bands inside and I made my way to the core. The core was a little hard ball of what appeared to be more rubber but of course I had to find out so I bashed the little ball with a rock. Something, either small bits of rubber or rock, came out of the smashed mess and ended up in my eyes. It was painful and I was running around yelling for Mum. A new and unusual injury for her to sort out. Just by myself I kept them both on their toes.

Most of the kids of this time were heavily into Cowboys and Indians. First Nation people now but in those old days of political insensitivity they were Indians or Red Skins. There was even a lolly bar called Red Skins. We were fed a constant diet of movies about the American West. Cowboys in white hats and their battles with the vicious savages who threatened the American way of life and their progress to taming the country. They fought terrible battles with the enemy, risking their very scalps while trying to established a good life in the Wild West. Stories of Gun Shooters and Sheriffs were told with awe in our voices Texas

Rangers, outlaws and the pursuing posse, all of these characters were soaked up and these stories filled our imaginations. In every backyard in Australia kids ran around in mock battle, the unlucky ones having to be the Indians and the bigger more popular kids were always in the leading roles of Sheriff or Ranger. I was just like every other kid. I was always running around shooting imaginary Indians.

While I was obsessed with these stories I begged Mum for a cowboy suit and she said she would make me one but for some reason known only to her, she made me an Indian vest and pants with lots of fringing. Maybe she saw through the stories and figured that there were heroes on both sides. I don't know. She made the vest from a pair of old sugar bags. It was bloody itchy. I was, however, determined to wear it and so with a chook feather stuck in my hair, I swapped sides. The Indians were now the good guys and the baddies were now the cowboys. This worked for me and, with great enthusiasm I ran around stabbing them and cutting off their scalps, scratching and squirming as I went. I made a great Indian or at least I saw it that way. I think childhood was mostly fun except for all the shit that happened.

At this time, I got the idea that I should have a pony, a real cowboy has a pony to ride. I was obsessed with the idea and pestered Mum and Dad relentlessly. We had horses on the property and Dad was a good rider. So I couldn't see why I didn't have one too. One day Dad called me and said, 'I've got you a pony. It's in the barn'. What! Really? I took off at a hundred miles an hour, raced into the barn but there was nothing like a pony in there. I raced out and yelled at him. He assured me there really was a pony in there so I went back in, unconvinced. There was no pony so I came back out, I was really mad now, yelling and screaming, all red in the face and close to tears. and he said 'come on I'll show you', he walked in with me and there it was, a pony. A pony made out of a 20gallon drum with 4 legs attached and a string tail. It had milk bucket for a head. Shit! Bastard! He thought this was funny but I didn't see the joke.

Dad did love to play tricks on us, it amused him to put 'one over our heads'. Once when he was drafting a mob of sheep he was separating some and I asked him why, he said they were pregnant and had to be dealt with differently. I asked him how he knew which ones were pregnant and he told me they had M on their foreheads. M for Mother. For several years after I still looked for the M. Before he killed a hen he would feel the chest, when asked why he said he was feeling for eggs. Didn't want to kill one and waste the eggs. I believed him of course and just accepted that was where you got the eggs from. I was only a little kid and Dad is Dad. Dad loved his jokes.

I ignored the stupid, metal pony and decided to ride the jersey cow instead. I was pretty good at this and was enjoying the fun of it when she up and dropped dead. Of course you know whose fault it was. It was my fault. To this day I don't know why she died but it was not my main concern which was I now had nothing to ride. During the days I was happily riding the cow I encouraged my little sister, (yes the one I took under the railway track), to try to ride the sheep. I would plop her on the back of one and it would take off, she would cling to the wool for dear life. The sheep always headed for the wool shed and the safety underneath. She inevitable fell off or got knocked off as they went panic stricken to hide under the shed. She still talks to me, occasionally. Usually to remind me of all the times I nearly killed her or got her in trouble. When we finally replaced our wire clothes line for the newly invented Hill Hoist I thought it was a playground for us kids. A swing and a merry go round in one. I remember hanging my sister on the line and running around spinning her as fast as my little legs could carry me. Mum and Dad surely knew it was me who broke it but they never said. I guess I could only be punished so much.

When we were kids we were expected to work on the farm and we did. There were always jobs, big and small. One of the weirder and crazy jobs I would do was to water divine. Somehow my Dad realized I had inherited my paternal Grandfather's gift and he was keen to use me to help him on the farm. He also saw the potential I had to bring in money so he would hire me out. I was pretty proud of this skill, for one it made Dad take notice of me more often and I also enjoyed the skill itself. I would walk around the paddock with the green wood stick, cut in such a way to ensure that there was a natural fork in it. I would hold each side of the fork and walk along. It would sort of feel like a pressure down my arms and when I was right on top of the water the stick would be dragged forcibly downward so much so that I did not have the strength to pull it back up. That's when I knew I had found the water. There was a certain pleasure in finding a water source. I used to be able to say how deep it would be as well. I don't know how much Dad charged for my services but none of it made it into my pocket.

I remember moving sheep from farm to farm, down the roads. We would walk behind the sheep hurrying them along and turning strays back to the mob. When I got tired I would hop up on one of the sheep and ride along till I thought that I had got the best out of that one and I would transfer myself to another one. I never got into trouble for this so I guess Dad had a bit of a sense of humour and he possibly admired my ingenuity.

I also remember that I loved to eat lambs' brains. When Dad killed a sheep I would immediately claim the head and splitting it open on the shopping block I would scoop out the brain and head for home. I was heading to Mum and the kitchen. She would usually cook them up for me right there and then as she was always in the kitchen anyway. All of us kids and a husband took a lot of caring for. She would roll and coat the brains in soft bread crumbs and then they would be fried in butter. I loved them. Years later in my fifties I felt the urge for those delicious lamb brains.

I went into the local butcher and asked him for the brains. He said, 'I don't keep them but will get some for you'. I ordered 10 brains. When I received them I couldn't contain my excitement, I quickly got some of them underway. I stored the rest safely in the freezer and prepared my feast. It was horrid. I felt sick and I was spitting it out and washing out my mouth. I immediately threw the rest in the bin and couldn't eat anything for ages. I visited the butcher later and he enquired about my feast. He had a good laugh at my expense.

One day I was coming home from school with my brothers and sisters, we all were running, fighting, throwing our school stuff down on the verandah and hoping for something to eat before going off to play when I realized that there were other people at our house This never happened and I was immediately on alert. Dad was home. Shit what the hell was going on. Subdued to silence I crept along the verandah to the door.

Inside the house Mum was sitting staring ahead of herself and Dad was standing behind her. She looked awful and was crying, tears were running down her face. Her nose was all red and she blew it a lot and wiped it constantly. She wiped at her face with her apron and looked at me. She shook her head and I walked back out the door. One of the ladies came out to us kids and told us Sam was dead. He's gone she said. We asked where but she said he was dead. It was hard to take and to understand. We were little kids and Sam was our baby.

Mum and Dad went with the police to the station to tell them what happened and Sam was taken away. I didn't look - I didn't want to see him.

When they came back, Dad dropped Mum off and didn't even stop the car and he was back down the pub, sucking up the sympathy and the free drinks. Bastard. Mum was still crying.

The next day it was over and it was like nothing had happened except for the big gaping raw hole in my heart that had held Sam in it. We didn't talk about Sam, Mum never mentioned him again or told us any-thing and Dad acted as if he had never even existed.

I think after that I just didn't care much at all about anything. Mum was a wreck and had drifted into auto pilot, she never came back to being herself.

A Confession

'Dad hated him you know. Couldn't stand the fact he was simple. He said it was my fault and that he wasn't having people talking about him and point- ing fingers. He said we had to go. All of us. He said either that or get rid of Sam

A few years later I was around 10 when Mum kept me home from school. She wanted to sit and talk with me, so I sat with her for a long time she told me about her life and how it had been living with Dad. Then she talked of Sam. 'Dad hated him you know. Couldn't stand the fact he was simple. He said it was my fault and that he wasn't having people talking about him and pointing fingers. He said we had to go. All of us. He said either that or get rid of Sam.' She had thought he meant a home but he told her he was not paying his hard earned money so some looney could sit around doing nothing for years on end. He just wanted him gone.

Sam my beautiful round smiling brother. Sam whose breath felt like angel wings on my face. Sam who I loved as much as I loved anything and more than I loved myself. I felt sick, I wanted her to stop talking but she seemed incapable of stopping - now she had started it all just spewed out of her mouth. She had smothered Sam. She waited until he was sleeping so that she didn't have to look into his beautiful, trusting eyes and see them change to fear and confusion She pushed the pillow over his face and held it there for an eternity. Then she lifted it up, placed it back beside him and went to bed. She said nothing and we all went off to school, as if tricking her own mind, she then went as if to get him up as usually and found him dead. If Dad knew he never said anything, I think he did. He was always going on about Sam. I think the police knew too. But what to do about it? He was simple, not worth much, a burden really, and they were good people and all those other kids needed their parents. Better to write cot death on the paper work and put it to the filing cabinet. I am not sure now, I blamed Dad at the time, but Mum didn't have to do it. She could have sought out some help, kids were put in homes. Maybe somewhere inside he reminded her of her own failure.

As an adult looking back at this time I am thinking to myself how does a kid of some 10years old digest this information? At the time I believed my Mum and I was pretty shocked and horrified by this confession. Why had she told me? Did she simply need someone to know? I wasn't scared of Mum after this but I knew instinctively not to say anything to anyone else. I have never forgotten the events of this day, of what Mum told me and how I felt. I think my elder brother may have known as much later in our lives I heard him talking to Mum and telling her if she did not stop her attempts to sell property left to me by my Dad then he would tell the police what he knew. I have always assumed he meant this incident but we never ever spoke of either conversation. I know I got my inheritance so she was definitely scared by what he had told her. Mum had spent a lot of the money Dad had left her. She had been given a lot and had wasted a lot.

Mum started going to church after Sam died and she decided I would be the one to go with her. She was probably trying to come to some peace with God or to assuage her guilt. Perhaps she really did believe in salvation and forgiveness, or maybe she was trying to fool herself and everyone else. At my childish age I didn't ask any of these questions I just accepted that I had to go with her so for now going to church on Sunday morning was what we did. Mum never did anything halfhearted and soon she was teaching scripture not only at the church but at my school as well, you can imagine the shit I got for this. This went on when I was in high school - there she was preaching to us all about the love of God and the value of the Church. Meanwhile I had joined the Church of England Christian Boys Club. I enjoyed this for a while but one of God's disciples, one of the ministers grabbed me and tried to molest me. I fought him and ran off and I never went back to the Christian Boys Club. Mum would come into my room and read me the bible at night, I hated this and going to the church where the

Minister was still working. I gathered the nerve and told her I wasn't going to church with her any more she was horrified and tried to force me to go but I was stubborn and did not give in. My church going days were over. I never told Mum or anyone else what happened with the Minister. I had told my parents things like this before and they had reacted by blaming me, telling me I was an embarrassment to them. Over the years Dad had certainly made me understand that he was not interested in any weakness, and that any acts of violence against me were my own fault.

A year after this Minister tried to grab me he was sent off to a new town and there he did successfully molest children. I found this out because after all these years he has recently been jailed for molesting children in the town he was sent to. One weird thing about him, one with no explanation, is that he would send me a Christmas card every year. I switch between good and evil intentions when I try to think why. Was he saying sorry or was he reminding me we had unfinished business. Either way I am glad he's in jail. The world is a better place for it, especially the kids. Would suit me if he died in there.

Money was always a problem for us kids when I was young, we never had any and always wanted some for something. We each got sixpence a week for pocket money. This was used for the pictures or for lollies and was usually spent on the day we received it. Back in those days you could get a lot more for sixpence but still it didn't really go far.

The highlight of our year was the local Agricultural show and we tried to save our pocket money for it, or find other ways to earn a bit of money. On the very rare occasion a circus came to one of the larger towns nearby you would need money to go and we had to have our own. Getting money was an almost impossible task but we found ways.

One, rather unpleasant, way was to pluck the dead sheep for the wool. This was a quite lucrative way to get money and I was keen to get to the 'dead'uns' before any of my siblings. I would listen closely when Dad said an old sheep was down in a back paddock, information like that was priceless and I always paid close attention to the conversations at the dinner table or when Dad came in at night. It was not an easy way to make money. You had to wait until the sheep was green and putrid, then you could pluck the wool with your hands. You would pluck as much as you could from the topside then try to roll it over. Grab a leg and pull, more often than not the leg came off in your hand and then you would have to get a hold of the smelly mess and try to roll it. Hard for a little kid. But I was also a most determined little kid and the reward was pretty good. Dad would have us bale the wool and then he would send it to markets as seconds. We usually got some coins, I can't remember how much, but it must have been worth it, for all the work and mess and smell we got in to collect the wool, as we continued to do this whenever possible.

Thinking of the shearing shed reminds me that we

had to work at shearing time, picking up the bits and pieces laying around and stuffing them into a bale. We would jump in to pack it down to get more in and more often than not we would fall asleep in there. It was soft warm and we were usually exhausted from the days' work. This would result in Dad screaming at us to, 'Wake up and get out. You little idiots. One day you'll get pressed for real, no saving you then'.

I have always been an inventive sort of person and always looked for the opportunities that came my way, especially when money was to be made. When I was a kid there was a lot of freedom and I was allowed to go off on my bike for hours on end without being questioned at all. One day I decided I would go diving for fish and shellfish, anything really and then sell my wares to the public. So I made my plans. When I had it all worked out I got my bike out and grabbed a bag for the fish, that I would just pick up off the bottom, and off I went. I would need the garden hose. I had to be sure Dad didn't see me take it. I rolled it up and put it across my neck and off I went pedaling down the road some 10 kilometres to the ocean. I finally got there and quickly got into the water, wearing my shoes and socks to save my feet from the rocks that would be on the bottom, where I would simply pick up the fish waiting for me. laying the hose out on the beach so that the end would be high and dry as I went under. I stuck one end in my mouth as the ocean closed over my head. I sucked hard on the hose and nothing happened. I tried harder but when I realized it wasn't working I spat the hose out. My feet began to float up. Consequently, I breathed in underwater and nearly drowned. It took me ages to get back to shore. Collecting my bag as it floated in on the tide I began the long journey home. Sad and deflated I abandoned the hose.

Dad was often heard to remark. 'There must be someone stealing hoses.' I often used the hose in some adventure. Once just to see what would happen I pushed the end of the hose down a rabbit hole on the lawn. Shoving it in hard I went to turn on the tap. Well we had great water pressure as the hose rapidly disappeared into the earth. I ran to turn off the tap and struggled to pull the hose out. No matter how hard I pulled it wouldn't budge. It must have been down thirty feet and I was simply not strong enough to get it up. I tried digging down but to no avail. I cut it off, filled in the hole and hid the rest. Poor Dad!

Some of my other money making ways were more successful. Catching and selling rabbits. They had not been subject to the eradication program that was soon to come and thus they were not poisoned then. The release of the Mixomatosis virus, an infectious disease, artificially introduced to reduce the rabbit population, worked very well. This was to stop the rabbits from destroying crops and native habitat alike but some people say to make us have to buy our meat and not live off the land. A lot of people did live off the land as money was scarce and times were tough, so not only was a rabbit good eating but caught and skinned and cleaned you could get $2.00 each for them. We trapped a lot and others we would shoot. I often went out rabbiting with my older brother and his new wife. He would drive and she would hold the spotlight. When we had a rabbit frozen in the headlights I would jump out of the vehicle and race after the rabbit, hitting it over the head with a poly pipe. More often than not I would not be completely out of the car and my brother would impatiently move closer to the rabbit and run over my foot as he went. I was too scared to tell him and he just yelled at me for not being quicker.

Another inventive way we had to catch rabbits was to run around an area filling in all possible rabbit holes in the warren and leaving only two unblocked. We would push a hose attached to the tractor exhaust down one hole and then wait outside the other one with a length of poly pipe and as they raced out we would bash them over the head and there you go, rabbit dinner.

At one point, when I was older I used to shoot or snare roos for pet meat. We did eat some of the meat ourselves. Mum always asked Dad for the roo's tail and she would make brawn. Once Dad was roo hunting from the back of his horse. He would gallop alongside and hit the roo with his stirrup, bringing it down then finish it off. One day he fell out of the saddle, unbalancing as his foot was out of the stirrup, and landed in a frenzied, tangled, mess with the roo. Of course the roo was terrified and fighting for his life so he was not going easy and immediately tried to rip his back legs into Dad. Lucky for Dad one of his dogs was alongside and he faithfully launched himself into an attack on the roo. He drove the roo off but got his guts ripped open in the process. His guts was falling out as Dad scooped him and his innards up and regaining the saddle he headed for home at a pace. When Dad got him home he deftly put him back together and sewed him up. He, miraculously, did survive. Dad probably shot him later.

As I grew older I came up with other means to make money, I would fish for salmon in the bay. I would stay out all night and fish by myself. I lit a huge fire on the beach for warmth and light and in the morning I would have to carry my haul up a steep cliff, often making six or seven trips as it was not unusual to catch thirty to forty salmon. During the night as I ran out of bait I would open the salmon to recover and reuse the bait. There were so many fish then, and no bag limits. I would take the fish off to Mt barker and sell them for $2.00 each. Those that had bites taken out of them from a passing shark, these I sold for $1.00 each.

I spent a lot of time as a youth trying to make money from all sorts of schemes. We had a few feral cats on the farm and often ten or twenty babies would be born. I would get paid sixpence each to kill them. I usually gave them a bash on the head. It sounds cruel now but back then I was more pragmatic. They were going to be killed so I may as well have my money. Dad eventually decided to castrate all the males which he did with sheep rings. One income source was lost.

When I was ten years old I used to do a milk run mostly just on Friday nights and sometimes on school nights as well when the old milkman couldn't make it on his own or a runner had let him down. Friday nights were pretty busy in our house cos Mum liked to go to the local hall for the dances. Dad didn't go and Mum was not permitted to go on her own so one of us kids had to go with her. Usually it fell to me to volunteer as everyone else wanted to run off to the pictures or to friends. I loved my Mum and going with her made it possible for her to go. So I did it. We had to walk to the hall. It was a 6kilometre round trip. We would be home by 10pm and I would sleep two hours and then get picked up at midnight. I would run the milk run until around 8am.

We were supposed to carry eight bottles as we left the truck. My hands were too small so Dad made me a wooden carrier to fit the bottles in. The old milko complained it slowed me down but he realised eventually that me making two trips back to the truck to get more bottles would be slower. Despite the fact this was exhausting work and I was up late almost every school night no teacher or Mum or Dad or relative ever suggested I was too young or too small to do the work. My pay for running the milk for eight hours was $2.00 or equivalent.

There were particular clients and houses that to this day I still feel the fear when I think about them.

One of the houses had a porch where a blue healer dog would lay on the mat under which the owner had put the envelope with milk money, either for safe keeping or to satisfy a warped sense of humour, the latter I think. When I took the money the dog would not move but would growl menacingly at me. We repeated this scenario every Friday. Another of these terrifying houses had a huge mummy in the hallway. I had to go into the house and put the milk on the kitchen table and pick up the money left there for us. I hated this house as it had a long dark hallway and I used to creep passed the mummy and then, when leaving, would run as fast as I could down the passage and out the door. I would be panting breathless on the steps. I often had to go into houses to collect money. Usually this was left on the kitchen table, you took the money, counted it, and left the milk. One old guy would have his milk left on the porch but then I would have to go inside and take the required amount of money from a jam jar he kept under his bed. Under that same bed where he lay sleeping, snoring and grunting with his mouth wide open. I was terrified he would wake up and get me. I would creep in, freezing in place at any variance in the noises and eventually get the money and high tail it out of there. Time lost getting in was made up on the way out.

When I got home often around 8am in the morning after being out since midnight, Mum would have a hot bath ready for me and I would fall in, dead tired. Often I would fall asleep in the bath and she would wake me for school. One day I found I still had money in my pocket. I told Mum and she said run and give it to him before school. He had a shop in town so I ran up. Instead of being happy and patting me on the back, he said, 'I thought money was going missing'. He was accusing me of stealing. He gave me the sack. A few weeks later he came to our house and asked me to come back and help him. I did. My Dad eventually bought a milk round and talked a few others into doing the same. I often helped them out, sometimes driving the truck myself. I was not yet fourteen.

When I was a little kid sometimes I would take a few coins, usually from my older brother's stash, as he was working now. He used to polish the coins and stack them up. I would then go to Mum and tell her I found it on the road or in town. She would say well you keep it for your honesty and I'm glad you told me about it. I often wonder if she knew this trick. She never said so.

I was constantly in trouble and I still got up to mischief but I wasn't the only hell raiser on the farm. I mention this just so you know I was not really any different to my older brothers. Just younger. One day my oldest brother, whose name I can't bear to say, wanted me to go bird egg collecting with him. I was the best tree climber because I was small. I could get up where they couldn't. Off we went. He decided to bring along the gun to get some rabbits. He was about 14 and I was 9. I was wearing a pair of trousers that were too big for me but you took what you could find in our family you were lucky to have a pair of pants to put on. They were made out of a very stiff material. Mum made all our clothes even made Dad's undies. I was struggling just to keep these trousers up. My brother got so mad at me because as I walked they were making a lot of noise as they rubbed together. He yelled at me to shut up and stop walking the way I was. 'Jee! 'Well I started walking along with my legs a few feet apart and this helped for a while. Unfortunately, you can't walk too far like this, so eventually the noise started again. He said if I didn't stop he was gunna shoot me. Shoot me! What! Over a squishy noise. I was a bit scared of him so once again I spread my legs way apart and started walking along, and once again it got to where I could no longer do this and the noise started. He raised the gun and pointed it at me. I took off and he shot. I heard the singing of the bullet and felt it go passed my head. I felt the wind of it on my cheek. Before he reloaded the gun I was down the hill across the paddock and under the bridge, hightailing it for home. I never mentioned this at home. No one would care. I just kept out of his way for a while. Talking about this makes me laugh now but I was not laughing then.

There were always jobs, big and small around the farm that had to be done. Some of these jobs were fun but some were really dangerous as it was proved without doubt in this horrible accident that took place on our farm some years before.

My oldest brother, yes him again, was driving the

tractor. I was 7 and he was 12. We were using the tractor and taking hay to the paddocks and feeding the sheep. Behind the tractor was a tray, that worked off the hydraulics of the tractor. I was standing on the tray, dressed only in my home made, red polka dot shorts. I had been pushing hay off the tray for the stock that followed along behind us like ducklings after their mother. The tray was now empty except for me and a pitch fork. He was driving too fast; He was a bit of a loose canyon was my big brother. He ran the tractor over a culvert and a vicious bump had me in the air, landing head first on the tray on the way down. My head was split open and I fell to the ground. My skull was cracked. and then as if the Gods just hated me, or my brother, the maniac, had planned it, the pitchfork came out of the trailer and speared through my face. It went in via my jaw and travelled upward, stopped only by my jawbone, before it would surely have killed me. I was covered in blood.

My brother did not know what to do. Mum and Dad were not home. No one was, just us. He shouldn't have been driving at all and was worried he would get into trouble if he took me to hospital in the truck. He was 12 years old. He was in a panic and there was an awful lot of blood, all over me and him. The hospital was about 70ks away. He decided to take me to our neighbor's farm for help and some adult advice. He put me in the truck and took me there. I was bleeding profusely from my jaw and my skull was fractured. When we got to the neighbor's they knew Mum and

Dad were in town so they decided to take me there to find them. They did find my parents and eventually I was taken to the hospital. I had cheated death by a mere fraction of an inch. The pitchfork's path was slightly diverted and had been slowed down by catching on my jawbone. This was enough to stop the fork from penetrating through to my brain.

Maybe it is this incident that helps to explain my hyperactivity, my being bored easily, and my lack of concentration and the constant seeking for new adventures. I've always desired change, something new and different. They didn't have a name to describe my condition when I was a kid. I was just considered naughty and unsettled. Me, I think it is just the way I was born as I had been up to all sorts of mischief long before I was seven but in spite all of this I was a smart kid and could do just about anything I set my mind to. I was always setting my mind to something.

One of the jobs Dad would have us help with was to burn off the stubble after harvest and before seeding. Dad had a great invention to help us get maximum results from our efforts. He had made these bent pipes about one-meter long which he filled with kerosene and stuffed the ends with old rags. When we got to the paddock he would set the rags alight and we would have to run through the stubble dragging the pipes along the ground, setting the grass alight as we ran around the paddock excited by the fire and the fun of it all. The stubble was hard and stiff and stuck us through our pants and socks, that's if we actually had shoes on, and we were often cut and scratched. Adding to the fun was the adrenaline produced by fear of getting burnt as everyone was out there starting fires and in general creating havoc. I don't remember any of us actually getting badly burnt or cut but we were lucky.

I always was trying to please my Dad. He would ask me to do something and because I was afraid of getting it wrong or making a mistake I would question him at length and try to get as much detail as possible to ensure I made a good impression. My efforts often made him lose patience with me and he would yell for my older brother and tell him to go and do the job. My brother would just go, he seemed to know what to do and how to do it. I just felt like shit and felt I would never add up to anything. I failed to understand that my brother was a good deal older than me and was used to working with Dad on a regular basis.

Dad

Dad was nearly 20years older than Mum and he was 50years old when I was born and I don't think he really had any idea what to do with me.

Dad was a small man, who definitely suffered from short man's syndrome. This resulted in him becoming a hard man as well. Despite all of this to me he was larger than life. I constantly sought his approval and attention. I didn't always get it and often when I did it was not what I had in mind.

Dad a short man with big ears and comb over hair. This is what I remember. I remember the hair as I got a comb tangled in it when I was practicing my hairdressing on him. I got an awful dressing down for this and was called every name under the sun. He never ever hit me though, or any of us kids, it was Mum who gave us the strap. Dad would often give us a kick if we weren't moving fast enough or we were in his way. He wasn't always gentle about that either.

Even though Dad had quit the pub an Italian friend would bring him port and he would take an occasional drink. One day when I was 15 the family went out so I set myself up in Dad's recliner chair and got out the port. Imagine how fast I moved when they came back unexpectedly. I left the port on the floor but he never said anything. I used to sit with him at night and do his corns for him, cutting them back with a razor blade so he did trust me to do something, or perhaps I was the only one silly enough to do it. As I have said before having Dad's attention or praise was a coveted prize. I would have done anything for him that's for sure

Dad would make me dress like a 100year old man. I often had my shoes either too big, to save money as I grew, or too small as they were hand me downs and would 'do me' for a while. My pants would be hand me downs from kids' years older than me. I remember as an older teen buying some stove pipe pants only to have Dad make me return them and get an old man's style, several sizes too big as well. It was hard to be cool with Dad around.

Money was a big issue with Dad, he was tight with it. He never bought new when old or recycled could be found. Perhaps this was part of living through the depression and having to go without, having to listen to his parents trying to find ways to feed the family. Perhaps he did go without as a child. I never knew because he never really talked to us at all. Or perhaps he was just a mean bastard.

Dad's need to recycle in order to save money, not the planet (we didn't know it needed saving then) often meant a straight forward job would quickly become a drawn out battle. He did things like recycle wire for fencing. Often we would struggle with a tangled roll of barbed wire before we could even hope to start working on the fence. Hours in time to save a few shillings, but as I said I did not know his past and what his circumstances were.

Dad loved to listen to the radio. We had a valve radio and at night the entire family would gather around the wireless and listen to Dad and Dave. After this we would all go off to bed. This was special time to me. Dad was happy and we were all together.

Music

I loved to play the drums and as a young child really enjoyed being able to do something really well.
Apart from the money which was great there were other reasons I loved being in a band. There were always girls around attracted to the music.
Girls loved bands. I loved girls.

When I was around ten years old I had the opportunity to learn drumming. What kid doesn't want to be a rock star? I began to learn how to play and I discovered a passion that was to last most of my life. I had lessons in the Army Drill hall with the Pipe Band. Mum used to walk me there twice a week for practice Thursday afternoon and Saturday morning. It was a long way about six kilometers for the round trip. I also played the piano at this time, I learnt this at school. Music was a joy and a challenge to me and I just seemed to 'get it' straight away. I constantly strove to be better, to learn more. I was a pretty good drummer and soon was in the school band. I was only 10 or 11 years old at the time. I later joined the Caledonia Pipe band and this was to continue right through till I was forty something. Later I was the

Drum Sargent for the branch and I also reached the position of District Chieftain. Not bad for an Aussie in a Scottish Band. Well that's what I think.

I guess we played a lot of music but we also drank a lot of whiskey, scotch of course. Sometimes we used to play on the road for dances and concerts and one time I remember being so drunk I could hardly hold the sticks let alone get ready. I was not the only drunk participant that night, the Drum Major had had his share as well. It was a Church social and as the curtains went up I felt the sling for my drum slipping, I asked for the curtain to be closed and did my best to fix it. The curtains rose we started playing, and my drum began slipping I just kept going down with it continuing to play as I got lower and lower. I call that real drumming skill. I remember I had a bit of a crush on one of the lasses in the band. I am not sure what my wife was up to but on one road trip she booked her and I in the same room. I was keen but she was not so didn't get to fulfil that fantasy. A few years later I heard from a mate that he had managed to taste the fantasized fruit and I was pretty pissed off until he admitted he was in such a state of excitement that he didn't last long and it was all a bit of a fizz. He was so embarrassed and she didn't come back for more. Life doesn't always deliver what you want but it's great for a good laugh at all and sundry including yourself.

I was, at one time, a drummer for the Police Pipe Band as well. I played at the Christmas Pageant in Perth with the Mass Pipe Bands. My life has taken some very weird turns. I don't play anymore, have not picked up a set of sticks for years. I wonder if I still have it? I probably do have it, why wouldn't I. Haven't forgotten much over the years. I have offered to help train the new drummers but in truth there are none. I think the band is done now.

My drumming abilities were well known in the town so it is not hard to understand that an up and coming rock band asked me to join them. I was 12 years old, I was a good drummer and they needed one. Problem was I was 12 years old and I was definitely not allowed in the pub. This was sorted out by a special dispensation from the Commissioner of Police. What he didn't know was that I was very nervous when I had to go into the pubs so the owners of the pubs would give me alcohol to relax me and most times I was playing drunk as a skunk.

During my apprenticeship years I played with a band in Coolgardie. I loved this because of the money I was paid. I received my board for the night and a meal and $300.00 for playing Saturday afternoon, Saturday night and the Sunday session. This was an awesome amount of money. My apprenticeship was paying around $12.00 per week.

As usually happens with me there is someone to spoil it My boss wanted me to work on Saturday mornings and if I wanted to eventually complete my apprenticeship I had to do so. I simple could not make the drive up to Coolgardie with time to do both the band and my apprenticeship. I had to quit the band

and all that money. Somehow at the time I had reasoned the apprenticeship was a better life plan. Did I make the right choice? Who knows I could be an aging rock star today if I'd made a different choice. I could have died as a result of a bad life choice too. Who knows.

Becoming a Man

Well I got my test results back and there is nothing
wrong with me they say. Can't explain it they say.
Oh well, it looks like I'm right for a few more years.
That's a good thing as I have a lot of things
to do, a lot of plans.

I was around 14years old I discovered all of the treasures and pleasures a girl had to offer and I was very quickly addicted. I couldn't get enough. I didn't have to be told to wash and I combed my hair and tried to get the better shirts before my brothers did. I wasn't tall and muscled like some of the boys but I was game and daring and did risky stuff. The girls at school liked this and I had my fair share of admirers.

At this time, I also discovered that the netball courts were a great place to find women, all shapes and sizes and all ages. All the boys knew this; it was passed down through the ranks. (Later I was to discover the nurses' quarters but that's another story). The courts, where the women and girls ran around in very short skirts with their knickers showing, were like a magnet to me. Those cute, fit, sporty women jumped around all the time happily showing off their underwear. I began to be a regular at the courts just watching the games. Well actually I was watching the women and mostly their crotches. Imagine what it would look like if they played without knickers. God It was wonderful. Unlike the nurses' quarters I did not have to contend with a grumpy middle aged matron catching me over and over.

I began to take notice of a particular woman of about 40 who often ran up close to me and would look at me as if she knew what was in, and on, my mind. She would bounce the ball in my direction and smile at me. She was a good looking woman and the fact she was years older than me was not a factor I considered. I'm not sure I even noticed, just those legs and those undies and what lay beneath.

One day after the game she asked me to walk to her car with her. I said sure, she asked me if I would like a ride home and of course I said yes. When we were both in the car she pulled her knickers off. 'They're wet' she said. I just watched, I had a huge erection, but I said and did nothing. I was thinking, 'Hell what if she notices,' She drove me home and went on her way. Driving without her undies. All that week I thought of her and dreamed of her. I dreamed of her sitting there without her undies in that little short skirt. I couldn't stop thinking about her when I was awake. I was in torment. I realised that I had made a very big mistake, I had been given an invitation that I didn't take. I was not going to miss that chance again. The next weekend there I was at the netball courts and there she was. After the game she repeated the invitation to walk to the car and of course I said 'yes.' This time I was ready. I was so ready.

We did not get out of the car park this time. The offer was made once again by the removal of the underwear and this time I did not hesitate; I took it wholeheartedly. We got into the back seat of the car, and I lost my virginity, in a car park, at the netball courts with a woman three times my age. Was I scared, no I can honestly say I was not. Was I excited? Was my heart racing? Absolutely both of these were true. I was ready, I had watched animals mating all of my life and I had looked a lots of forbidden porn magazines. I had listened in to the conversations of my older brothers and had long and earnest discussions with kids during school and hanging around town. Talk was all we had and we made the most of it but today that was going to change for me.

Once more she was without her knickers and she lay back up against the corner of the back seat. She parted her legs and I saw the Holy Grail. I had a very urgent need to get myself inside. With her help I guided my throbbing, about to explode, cock in to her. She wrapped her legs around my back and I was in heaven. All of my senses were concentrated on the soft and warm cocoon that I slid in and out of. She was hot and wet and so soft, I was in heaven. I think I came within about two seconds much to my own disappoint and her amusement

She asked if I would like to drive back with her to

her home I said yes. We repeated this pattern often and not just on weekends. She was very demanding sexually and this suited me fine. I realised I was too. She was horny most of the time. So was I, a perfect match. We often had to stop on the side of the road so I could satiate her appetite before getting home. She was married and the word on the street was that her husband was pretty sure there was a man on the scene and he searched that small town on a deadly mission. Lucky for me he never suspected a kid from another town. I don't believe he ever found out just what his wife was, and who, she was doing. Our dalliance lasted about 18th months I had discovered other girls and I think she became bored. Maybe I was out growing her requirements. We saw each other less and less until we stopped. At the time I assumed I was the only one enjoying her favours but who knows. It was to be 4 years before a chance meeting had us doing it all again. It was still very good.

The time I spent with her was delightful, I was invited and encouraged to explore and enjoy what and where and how I liked and I did. A kid in a lolly store. Practice makes perfect they say and I became very competent in getting the best out of myself and pleasuring her as well. I discovered early I could come more than once and often enjoyed a fuck that lasted hours. I've learned since that this is not the normal way for a man and I've also learned the ladies love it. Satisfaction all round. Well that's the way I see it. No one has complained then or since as to my peculiarity in this. She taught me how to please her and how to tease. She helped me navigate the female body and find ways to give her pleasure and to take it for myself. I was 14 years old and I had discovered the joy and beauty of a woman who is comfortable in her own skin and enjoys herself sexually. I can't count the woman I've had since but I have loved them all. Even the ones who paid me.

* * *

I love women. I love everything about them. Their hair their faces their mouths, the way they walk and talk. I love the flirty ones. The ones who like to be provocative. I like the ones who you know want to get it on the same as you but they make you play the game. I like my women all shapes and sizes but most I love the ones with a bit of weight on. The big thighs as they wrap around me the soft feel of their bum as you get a handful of it. Women! I love them all.

One day my Mum came home unexpectedly and I had a girl in my room. A girl in my bed actually. At the sound of the front door she jumped up and hid in the wardrobe. Naked. Mum walked in the room, never glanced at me but strode purposely toward the wardrobe. I was shocked, staring, what the hell was she going to do. I jumped up as she reached out and locked the wardrobe pocketed the key and walked out. She never said a word and neither did I. After she left I had to find something to prise the wardrobe door and let my friend out. I didn't ever get to finish that business but a few years later this girl asked me to go to the Doctor's with her as she thought she was pregnant. She was scared so I agreed to go with her for moral support. The old Doctor tore strips off me for several minutes before I could get the words in to say it was not me and not my baby. What a lecture. In truth I deserved the lecture cos I had taken a chance many times. Many years later, working in a village community a woman came up to me and asked if I could do some work for her when I had finished the job I was there for. She was about to tell me her name when I said, 'I know you, last time I saw you, you were naked, hiding in my wardrobe,' she recognized me and we had a good laugh at all the things that had happened to us over the years.

* * *

It was because of this love of the female form in all of its shapes and sizes that I decided to join the surf life savers. I loved water, rivers and ocean. I loved the surf boats. We would go out in the surf boats to force sharks away from the beach, it was great fun, Exhilarating! But my main motivation was the women in their bikinis. Lovely. There was a particular woman who would come to the beach a lot. She had a little baby that she played with in the surf. She wore a tiny black bikini which showed of her beautiful body, her boobs were delicious. Lovely big and soft. White in the sun. When I was in the tower, instead of watching the swimmers, I sought her out on the beach. One day in heavy surf she was hit by a large wave and lost hold of the baby. We all rushed into the water to help find the child. We couldn't see a thing. Lots of froth and white water. Then I felt something bump up against my leg. I instinctively reached in and grabbed and I got hold of the baby by its fat little leg and I pulled him out. He was fine and I was in heaven, hugged tightly to those lovely, warm breasts. This was a great day.

Not all days were the same and the next day things were not as wonderful. Our team was practicing in the big heavy surf boats when the order came to ship oars. Well I didn't manage to ship mine and almost decapitated the rest of the crew. It didn't go down too well as they all flung themselves to the floor. No sense of humour. I didn't last long in the life savers. Mainly over enthusiasm got me, I think.

I have actually saved a few more lives in my days at the beach. It was up in Exmouth and I was just lazing on the beach when I noticed a man floating along in the current. He seemed to be rolling over from back to front and just enjoying himself. As I watched him I realized his actions were peculiar and I thought that maybe he was in trouble. I watched him a while longer and I saw that he was barely moving so I jumped up and into the water and I got out there as quickly as I could and dragged him in towards shore. At this point I was helped to get him in by another man who was watching from the beach, he and I performed CPR on the drowning man. When he finally regained his normal breathing and was recovering he said his snorkel had malfunctioned. I am not sure exactly how this would happen, and he had become exhausted. He was a Polish tourist and I had been watching him drown, thinking he was having fun. Well I did redeem myself by saving him.

Another incident occurred on a holiday in Kalbarri I had been skin diving off my boat when I came across a tiger shark that was on the bottom of the ocean. I came back up and got out of the water. I was not sure what the shark was doing and thought he may be dead but I was not going to take the risk. I noticed a lady swimming in the area directly above the shark. I called out to her partner who was still in their boat to tell him about the shark and then I noticed the woman was having a fit in the water and then sinking. I dived into the water and dragged her to the boat where her partner helped to get her on board. He did not jump in the water to help which seemed a little odd at the time. She had had a heart attack. I often wonder if she saw the shark but I never got to ask her. She was taken away in an ambulance and I was later told she had survived.

I loved the ocean and the rivers. I loved boats and pretty much everything about waterways, rivers and oceans. Later in my life I was to own several different boats at different times. There was one I especially enjoyed. I lost that in my second divorce settlement.

I still enjoy being on, in or near the water. I have a little boat now. I take it out fishing, I take my two little dogs with me. We all have life jackets and most of the time I get the helm but sometimes one of the dogs claims the driving seat and because I'm such a softie I let him have it. I enjoy fishing. Seafood is a source of income and food that costs only your effort to produce.

As a teenager and a young man I would help the men to run the nets. We would drag the nets out into deep water and leave them sit for a few hours then drag them in. A few of us would get out behind the nets as they were pulled in. Our job was to allow bull sharks out of the net as we came up to them as their weight would break the net. they would flash past us as they escaped into deeper water. Never really considered myself in danger. Escape was on their minds not dinner. I often fished to make extra money selling it all to restaurants and locals on the quay.

I was about 17 when I took up boxing I was a little guy but I was tough and I was sick of being picked on. Especially by my older brothers who were a constant pain to me. The oldest one in particular. Not sure what it was that he hated about me but he certainly gave a good indication that he did. He taught me a lot about life and farming, but mostly he taught me how not to be a prick.

* * *

I really got good at boxing. I loved the raw energy, and the power I felt when I was belting someone. I even liked belting the bag, pretending it was Dad or my brother. I learnt to box at the Police and Citizens Club. This was a place where cops worked with kids in sporting endeavors. It was a public relations exercise and was supposed to keep us off the street. This didn't work with me but for a few years it did. It did help me later though as the cops all knew me and went a little easier on me I think. Boxing was big on the agenda in every PCYC and I competed across town and the state.

Before a fight I was pumped with adrenaline, I was ready to go and I wanted the fight, perhaps I needed it. During the fight my focus was intense and everything around me disintegrated into the necessary and the unnecessary elements. My world was the sixteen by twenty feet of the ring, inside the ropes and the two of us. A pantomime, acted out in time that appears to have slowed down. Everything is exaggerated, every movement, every punch, every advance and retreat is seen and felt and anticipated, rejected and enforced with a cold calculated precision. The ring itself was either too big or too small depending on your status, too small when you're taking a beating and too big when you're in control. Pain in the ring is not felt like it is after when you look in the mirror and see the wounds. There is no adrenaline now to act as a salve, to numb the pain. The pain that in the ring is a motivator, a friend, now hurts you like hell.

I took great pleasure watching the kids come up to the ring to fight. I could see their smirks when they saw me - the little guy - I could read their minds. This was going to be easy. It'll be over within minutes. I could sense their satisfaction, that smug feeling when things are going your way, when you think your opponent wont measure up. You think you will get out of the ring unscathed and an easy victory is on the table.

I took even more pleasure when that look of confidence changed to confusion and fear as I danced around the ring, untouched by all their efforts to land one on me. When I saw my chance I walloped them with an uppercut straight under the jaw. A joy to behold. The shock in their eyes, the backward snap of their ugly heads, the sweat mixed with spit and blood flying as mouth guards were spat or knocked out. The rush when I connected and the anticipation of the fall. I never danced until the count was over, I never claimed my victory till the referee raised my hand but I was sure of it from the moment I saw my smug opponent's guard fall and I moved in for the hit.

Boxing was a great sport for me. It was individual and I was used to relying on myself. It gave me more confidence, possibly not a good thing. Boxing also helped me with a bit of extra money. I was doing my apprenticeship by now and the pay was 12.00 per week. There was a boxing troop in town. They set up their tents and rings and stayed around as long as the punters came to watch and spend their money. Most of the fighters were black. Mostly they were great fighters, but I was better, I knew how to fight in the ring. I knew when and where to use my energy and when to stay out of the way. I never wasted a punch.

I liked to get a knockout early in a fight, no sense in getting hit if you didn't have to.

The great part about the troop was they were always looking for punters to come in and have a go. $20.00 if you could last three rounds or if you achieved a knockout before that. Their money was made by running a betting ring. They never really expected it to happen but I was soon earning my money and enjoying it. I never mentioned any of it to Mum or Dad mostly because she would not have approved and he wouldn't have cared. I never told my friends either but this was because I did not want to be embarrassed if one of the fighters did happen to get me. None of them did. It wasn't without trying and cheating and sometimes a second man would jump in the ring behind me and I'd have to take both of them on. I remember one occasion, makes me laugh now, when a second fighter had jumped in with me and an off duty policeman jumped in the ring and took him out of the equation. Fair's fair I guess was his reckoning I thought at the time but I also think he may have had his money on me.

Not long after I started boxing I was winning almost every fight and I was cocky. One night at a training bout my trainer gave me a beating. I still haven't forgotten. Later he came up to me and said I'm sorry Rob but you needed that. If you get to big for your boots and too cocky you will make mistakes. I understand that I probably did deserve it but if I ever get a chance to even the score I would very much like to do so. It is unlikely as he is probably dead now or so old I would not be able to do it. Maybe I'm too old now but I don't think so.

I continued to box and win awards into my adult years. There have also been quite a few unofficial ones for sure, most I didn't want but some I went looking for. I hated injustice and I hated if someone picked on those that couldn't defend themselves. Animals, women, kids anyone who was vulnerable. This is what I tell myself but maybe I just like the fighter in me a little too much. A lot of these out of the ring fights were because of Mum and some when I was part of a motor cycle gang (I use the word lightly) which took its fun by picking on surfers. We did not always come out on top with the surfers. Well I did but some of the others were not so fortunate.

Many years later, caught in the wreckage of a very dysfunctional relationship, I was to have my last fight. I was a broken man at that point, struggling to have any self-esteem or self-confidence. I felt old and use-less. I was lying in my bed struggling for a good reason to get up, and reading the local paper, I saw the ad-vertisement for challengers for a boxing match in the Southern suburbs of Perth. They were to be the lead up to a bigger match. I was still registered as a boxer and I wondered if I still had it in me. I thought I must have, there's not much else. I called and got an inter-view. Off I went, bluffing my way as usual, lying about my age of fifty-three to get passed the rules. I hadn't trained in the ring for years but I was fit and strong.

I wanted to do this. To prove something just to me. I thought it would help me to feel more like I used to. I wanted to feel like I was the one in control, the one that made the rules. I wanted to hit someone.

Leading up to the fight I was filled with regrets and for the first time ever I felt nervous. My opponent was much younger and was keen, had been training and was eager and fresh. I on the other hand was unprepared and wishing I'd not been so stupid but here I was and I would fight. That's me. I stepped into the ring and the old focus found me. I remembered the way to fight and it all flowed back. I looked for his weaknesses as I always did. I relied on this, his weaknesses not my own strength. I won the fight on points. I was not as happy as I thought I would be. I was hurting and had taken a beating in the process of winning. I went home and looking in the mirror at my bashed and bruised face. I felt like shit. I felt old and stupid. It had proved nothing except maybe I was an idiot. I never fought in the ring again. I have been involved in a few street fights but never ones I wanted to be in or that I have caused. I will walk miles and do all I can not to fight these days.

A few years after I started boxing Dad died and even though I had spent most of my years hating him I felt he had softened a little over the years, but in truth I still feel a bit disappointed in him. He was an arrogant, unfeeling man and yet somehow I managed to love him in my own way. When he had the stroke that was to take his life I would walk miles each night to go to the hospital to see him. Even then he wouldn't lend me the car.

When I was a little kid I used to pretend that I was Huckleberry Finn and I tried to base my life on his. I found my own role model when none was offered to me. Later in my life, a grown man finding myself alone once again, I discovered Peekay in Bryce Courtney's master-piece, The Power of One, and I chose to see myself like him. Just me against the world. I actually feel that way now but now I'm good with it. I like it. I depend on myself and, apart from my dogs, no one depends on me, so in a way, I am totally free. Free to go and come. Gets lonely sometimes though.

I felt Mum would be better off with Dad gone. Unfortunately, she really wasn't. He had beaten her down, broken her emotionally and she never understood her own worth. She became a bit of a whore in truth, always on the lookout for a drink and a man to warm her bed. To take the edge off the emptiness of her life. The words in her head.

Mum had done her best for a while but when the older kids left home she began this sad way of living. I was a married man now, so I had a bit more of an understanding of what was going on. Mum fell deeper and deeper into herself and seemed only alive when she was getting ready to go to the pub for a few. Many a man who didn't treat her right ended up on the end of my fist and I became a bit like the enforcer for all our family ails, punching the lights out of anyone who crossed us. Years earlier Dad had asked me to go and sort out a man who was cheating with my oldest brother's wife. This man involved in the cheating still lived with his mother. I went around to the house and had a word to his Mum, a woman in her late 60's. She made me a cup of tea and we sat together chatting away till he came home. She knew her son was going to get beaten up but she felt he deserved it.

Career

I've done lots of different jobs and now I'm doing not much at all. Well that's not exactly true. I am building my own home, a place to be when I'm not out in my van. I'm just setting my place up and pretty much doing as I please. I like it this way. I've been asked to go here and there and work another few year, but I don't think I'm going. Yes, a bit more money would be good but truthfully I can't be bothered. I have my boat, my van, my little place here on the farm. I go where I want to, fish when I feel like it.
I have my kids close by.
No I won't be going back to work.

I was still at school and trying to work out what I wanted to do when I finished. There was a hairdressing course at the TAFE and we were offered it. It was a no brainer really, you got out of school and most of the participants were girls, so where else would you rather be? In truth though I actually enjoyed working with people's hair and had been made an offer to work at a local salon as a trainee I was considering when Dad stepped in and told me I had to stop hairdressing. 'Why?' I asked perplexed. I was actually doing something that I enjoyed and that I was halfway good at. 'You'll turn gay' he said, 'and no son of mine is going to be gay'. There was little point in arguing with my Dad. I gave up hairdressing. I'm not gay. Maybe I should have told him about my lady friend, the net-ball player who liked to drive without her knickers, but no, not taking the risk of ending that relationship was I.

So I had to reconsider. I was not great at school, not because I couldn't learn but because it didn't interest me. The world was full of life and excitement that I needed to feel and explore. School was just a waste of time. I was good at woodwork and metal work. I loved creating things. I was good with my hands. Many of my school projects graced the display cabinets in the foyer at the school but not one had my name on display. Still don't know why. Ashamed to admit that I was good at something I guess, who knows the petty mind of a small town school principal. I was then offered an apprenticeship at a carpentry shop in town. Someone who knew Dad arranged it for me so finally the old bastard was of some value. The best part of it all was having a place I liked to be. I remember the smell of the place, the scent of the wood, freshly cut. The way the old guys teased you and swore when something went wrong or right. The sounds of the place and the comfort of losing yourself in what you were doing. I was 14years old and I was on my way. Later in my life as a highly qualified carpenter, winner of various awards, I was to meet one of my old school wood work teachers. He asked me if I could take him on as a student to teach him some of the new methods and innovations in carpentry and of course I agreed to do so. The first day he came in I grabbed him by the ear and twisted it hard. At his astonished and annoyed retort, I simply said that's what you did to me every day at wood work class at school. Eventually he saw the humour and had a good laugh. We then got on with the work at hand.

In a variety of workshops across the city and across all of the trades the apprentice sweeps the floor and gets the lunches for a year or so before they actually get to work on their own and with the tools. This place put me straight on the tools. I loved that. Was I too cocky? I don't know, I don't think so. I always did it by the rules and carefully followed the instructions given to me. About 4 weeks into my apprenticeship I was alone in the workshop and had the task of putting braces into a table. I had successfully managed to plane and fit two of the braces but the third one was stubborn and I put it back in the machine to take 'a tiny bit more' off the bottom of the brace.

In these days there was not a lot of emphases on safety and the machine had no guards or safety switches but I doubt any would have saved me. The wood was tough and perhaps the machine was out of whack but the wood vibrated violently and the brace slipped and my hand followed through into the machine.

In shock and on my own, my only coherent

thought was that I had to get home. Get to Mum. She would know what to do. I raced outside and grabbed my bike. The bike was too big for me and I was always a bit unstable on it but today I was really unstable, one hand bleeding profusely, fear cursing through my veins and trying to go fast all at once. Home was only a kilometre away but I didn't make it. I fell off the bike directly into the path of a vehicle. Fortunately for me he was able to stop in time and didn't add to my injuries. He got me into his car and he raced me to the hospital.

I was holding my hand in my lap, still wearing my leather apron so that when we arrived at the hospital, immediately I saw the emergency sign, I jumped up to get out. I still remember the blood. Blood everywhere. Blood sheeting over the windscreen covering the interior of the car. There was so much blood that it was only years later it occurred to me how much of a mess I had made in his car. I was simple concerned only with my pain, my need for Mum and the doctors to help me. I was terrified I would lose my hand or my fingers.

It would be two years before I met this stranger and thanked him for his help that day. He knew who I was and he spoke to me, asked do you remember me? Of course I did. I said yes and he asked to see my hand. Didn't look like that last time I saw it. Never seen so much blood! He said.

At the hospital they put me immediately to the operating theatre and when I came to my hand was heavily bandaged. All of the staff kept reassuring me. Everything's alright. You'll be okay. Don't worry. I took this to mean what I wanted it to mean and that was that my fingers were not lost that my hand was intact. I was devastated when the bandages came off and the top half of all of my fingers was missing. My thumb was intact.

I slumped around for weeks, I was in shock at first and eventually the shock wore off and the physical pain was bearable, then gone altogether, but I was in deep depression. How was I going to cope in life without my hand? It was the old Doctor that set me straight, gave me a right dressing down. His words cut me but he was not 15 years old, still a kid really, and without the maturity to see that it was not so bad. 'Stop moping around feeling sorry for yourself. Grow up. There's nothing wrong with you. There are hundreds that have lost eyes and legs, those that can't move. You get back to work and snap out of it'. I did try to snap out of it but as I said I saw it as a major defect and something to be ashamed of. I did go back to work.

Snapping out of it, accepting the fact that I now had no fingers, was easier said than done. A lot of people, mostly girls, young teenagers would take delight in teasing me. Inane! Nasty! Hurtful! I found all of this pretty upsetting, partly because of the teasing, but also my own insecurities and beliefs that somehow the loss made me less of a man. I had this amazing idea that I should start wearing gloves when I went out. This idea was inspired by the popular TV show The Avengers and its star character, John Steed. He wore black leather gloves that were upmarket and manly. No one laughed at John, how could they laugh at me.

I wanted black gloves just like him but of course these were not available to me but I did find a pair of white cloth ladies' ones. Not quite the same but still an improvement on the no fingers look I thought so I decided to wear them anyway. I wore these gloves when I went out at night and one night the local police noticed the gloves and grabbed me. 'What have you been nicking they asked.' 'Nothing. I've lost my fingers so I wear the gloves to hide it, ' 'Take them off and show us.' I was so upset and felt humiliated by this injustice but they gave me no choice and I had to submit.

The truth is I was embarrassed by my missing fingers. I still am. It's like a bit of you is gone and everyone notices. But in truth no one did and years later I went through an entire army medical without anyone noticing this. It never actually stopped me being the best carpenter in the whole of the region, 23 awards in total. I won tradesman of the year three times in a row. My missing fingers were only ever an issue in my own head. Even now though, all these years later, I'll unconsciously hide my hand.

One of the carpentry awards was a cricket bat signed and presented by Merv Hughes. On the night I received it someone at the dinner asked to buy it from me for $4000 as I wasn't a cricket fan, but I said no. Now it's out in the shed, waiting for me to run out of firewood, I laugh and say when anyone asks me where it is. I probably would burn it you know; I don't have much need for such personal affirmations these days. I did display it for a while though, along with the other awards but now it doesn't seem to be of any significance. Life goes on.

The business that had employed me at this time had failed to add me to their insurance and I was not covered by any worker's compensation because of his error or sloppy administration practices. So here I was, half my hand gone, the memory of the pain and the fear I felt and now I would not get paid for the time I was off work and no compensation at all. To this day I am still traumatized and can't bear to see any sort of blood and gore without being transported back to that day. An injured terrified kid that just wanted to get to his Mum. I was not lost as Dad went to bat for me and he was at his best when he knew he was in the right and soon was offered $900.00 for my injuries and loss of fingers. Dad would not accept this and he asked for more on the grounds that I used to play the piano and this would not be possible anymore. I really didn't like learning the piano, mostly because of the teacher and the distance travelled for lessons. On foot as Dad would never let mum drive the car without him. It is unlikely I would ever have been a great pianist but it got me a further $300.00 added to the offer and Dad accepted it. I had to wait until I was 21 to receive this money. It was invested for me and a grand sum of $2200 was waiting for me when I survived to the age of 21. This was a considerable amount of money at this time especially if you lived an impoverished life like I was.

An incident that took place sometime later remains in my mind. An older man who was working alongside me was in too much of a hurry one afternoon and he fed the wood into the machine without someone on the other end. He put his hand behind to guide the wood and I, standing beside him, was waiting for instructions, I knew exactly what was going to happen seconds before it did. He chopped the fingers off his hand. He was rushed over to the first aid station before being taken to the hospital and the Boss picked up the old guy's fingers and in some twisted attempt to make us feel better he gave them to him. At this macabre site I promptly fainted and the old guy did too. He went to hospital and I went home. The next day he returned to work, not being able to afford the time off and I stayed home too shook up to work.

A few years later I was to catch my index finger in a docking saw. I was helping the Boss to fix something with it. I was under the bench threading a screw back in when he lost his temper with the saw and ripped the machine out of its housing. Unfortunately, my hand was attached and my finger ripped to the bone. This time it was reattached and sewn up. When I came back from the hospital later that day I found my Boss outside attacking the offensive machine with a hammer. In my innocence I thought he was making sure it didn't get someone else but in truth he was making sure Worksafe had no case against him when they came around.

Toward the end of my apprenticeship my numbers came up in the draft. Well that's what we thought from the papers. My Dad rang me at work and said, 'your numbers came up'. National Service. I was happy. My Granddad had fought in the war, 1st World War. I admired him. Grandad had given me a shell from the war and it was my pride and joy until a few years later the army arrived to collect it. It was still armed.

I was keen to go and Dad replied to the letter saying I was on my way. At the appointed time I was flown out from Perth to Puckapunyal in Victoria. I was 20, keen to defend my country and I knew I would not get anywhere if they saw my fingers so I simply never showed anyone and went to great lengths to hide my hand. I passed my medical and the first day my hair was shaved off, my balls cradled, and uniforms distributed. The second day it came to the notice of the officials I had not completed my apprenticeship I had not actually been called up at all but Dad had read it that way. The Army had brought me to Puckapunyal as they read from the letter I was volunteering. I was sent home to complete my apprenticeship, and to await notice in two more years. Geoff Whitlam became Prime Minister and I never got to go back.

Reminiscing about this trip to Puckapunyal I remember Dad driving me up to the airport and that Dad showed his emotions about me going to the Army. This was the only time I saw my Dad cry. This was an adventure for me, also my first airplane flight and I found all of this exciting. I didn't think much about Dad's emotive farewell till later.

Perhaps Dad's crying was more about his remembering my first military experience than sadness at my departure. I was about 12 or 13 when I joined the Army Cadets attached to our local school. How proud I was. I had my boots shined to a high gloss the night before cadets. I walked to school careful not to mark them. The kid at school who were not cadets would chase us around and step on our boots. Even though we would try we would often get called out over our boots. No amount of protesting convinced the trainers that we were powerless to do anything about the bullies. I loved my uniform. Khaki, big, rough, itchy and I was in heaven when I wore it to school.

One day we were holding an Army Cadet demonstration. Patents and grandparents and local dignitaries had all turned out for the day. We had formed two teams to display our formation and fighting skills. I was in charge of firing the mortar which was a blank but still flew through the air and made a bit of noise. It was a signal that the battle was about to start. I was to point it away from the other team and to shoot it backwards away from us and the rest of the school and the parents and officials who were watching. Well that didn't make sense to me. Why was I shooting backwards? It was a blank. It wouldn't hurt you if it flew over your head anyway. So I adjusted the aim and pointed it in the direction of the other team. I was careful to aim it high - way above their heads and off down the oval. They were all lined up holding their weapons and bayonets and standing so proud and determined to make a good display when the 'war' started. All of the spectators were sitting happily awaiting the games. I fired the mortar. It was an incredible scene of mayhem. Kids running screaming in all directions as the mortar went buzzing over their heads. Students and teachers grabbed each other and ran for the buildings, Mums and Dads panicked and tried to find their own child in the melee that followed. I just stood there. Partly proud, partly terrified but mostly highly amused.

Of course no one was hurt, well not physically. No one saw it like me. The best fun any of us had had in months. No! I was told I was discharged from Army Cadets and asked to turn in my uniform. I was devastated. I was looking forward to the camp, that was to be held in Northam later that year, with cadets from all over Western Australia. In my eyes I was a hero. I had routed the enemy, won the war, and all without any loss to either side. Instead of a medal I was asked not to come back. Life's funny isn't it.

So you see Dad may have been sad to see me go or he may have been fearful of how I would handle it all, whether I may blow something up. Maybe he was sad to see me go or he was worried for me and how I would cope with a second rejection. Anyway as I said it never came to that, once more my military career was cut short.

In the last year of my apprenticeship I had to move to a town a few hundred miles away as there was nowhere local to finish the course. The apprenticeship board, in agreement with me and the employer, took away the credits for one years of work and study. This deduction made it more affordable for the new company and they agreed to take me on. This added an extra year to my apprenticeship. I wanted to finish and to have work and it seemed that this was the only way so I went along with it. It was this extra year that got me out of the army. So good or bad luck I'm not so sure. My life was pretty tough, I had very little money and nowhere to live. The Boss said I could sleep in the old shed at the back of the block. It was an old tin shack, no floor and the walls were full of holes and cracks, there were no windows, no furniture and no bed.

From having nothing to having nothing wasn't a great journey so I began to look around for what I would need to stay in the shed. I found an old bed frame at the tip and from then on I set about building my room. I eventually had it set up with a little table and wash stand, a place for food, and a chair. I put some timbers down for a floor and plugged up the holes to at least try to stop the freezing winds whistling through at night. It did make it warmer. It was freezing in winter and a furnace in summer and there was no such luxury as electricity, it just was what it was. I used candles for light and had an outside fire place for cooking. I mean a drum with a fire in it. I was always a neat person and I kept everything tidy and in its place. I could lock it up and I had a place for myself. I thought it was okay. Poverty leaked from its walls and into me but I held fast to my apprenticeship and continued to lose myself in the workshop. The place I loved.

During this time, I kept pretty much to myself, having little money to go out anywhere. Women and taking them out cost money and I had none so this part of my life was also on hold. For four years I never had a girlfriend and thus had no sex, well not with a partner anyway. One of the people that worked with me was a lovely young woman that I liked a lot but her Mother was very quick to warn me off and made it very clear her daughter was not for me.

I finished my apprenticeship and returned home and soon after I met and married my first wife. It just seemed to be what you did. I look at the sequence of events that led up to this. I had met my sisters friend while home for a few days during my apprenticeship and I really liked her I think I may have actually loved her. I returned to my work and we had an agreement to wait two years and when I finished I would return and we would get married. I returned but she hadn't waited and was already married with a baby in tow. I was heartbroken. Devastated! At this time, I went up to Manjimup on a building site for a couple of weeks.

There I met my soon to be wife, it was only about six weeks later we decided to get married. I think I had had in mind for so long that I was getting married I just wanted to do so. We had a church wedding. At first the Catholic Church rejected the idea as I was not Catholic so I said okay stuff it we'll get married in a registry office and they relented allowing the marriage as long as I promised to bring my offspring up Catholic. I agreed with my fingers crossed behind my back. We decided to get married on a Friday to keep the costs down. It was Friday the 13th. Not many people would be able to come on a Friday. Everyone would have to work. The wedding was small only about 20 people. My wife wore a traditional wedding dress in white and my brother and his wife were our Best Man and Matron of Honour. I remember I wore a white suit and white shirt and a purple bow tie. Not sure what I was saying with this outfit but I definitely was not declaring my virginity. That was a long time gone. I am sure I was the handsome devil I thought I was but can't prove it now as the photos never turned out. Don't ask family to do the wedding pictures. It doesn't work. Maybe it was an omen. I didn't feel anything spectacular or emotional on my wedding day, just an ordinary day, going about business, getting on with life. Maybe a little more boring than usual.

* * *

During the short time from meeting my soon to be wife and getting married her Dad asked me to join the Buffalos club. I joined to please him. The week I was to be initiated he got sick and I had to stand on my own. I was terrified, worried about what was to happen, some stories said I would have to ride a Billy goat or worse, I thought I was not going to get through it in one piece but when it was all said and done I was to give a speech. No idea what it was about but it lasted about 30 seconds and I was in. I was given a clay pipe as a symbol of something and just when I went to take it the master broke it in half. I was a bit bemused, never got the significance but then we had dinner and a piss up. One of many piss ups to come. My membership status allowed us to hold our wedding reception in the Buffalo's Hall. My Father in Law was to die a few months later and without him I stopped going to the meetings, I did it to make him happy and he was gone.

The money that I was awarded for my accident back when I was 14 had been put aside for me and it had increased in value to around $2200.00. A small fortune in my world. I used it now to put a deposit on our first home and to buy some furniture. Good came from bad, I lost my fingers but I could get my first home. Despite this windfall I was soon running around in a bit of a panic as to how I was going to pay my mortgage on my salary and this feeling got worse when I discovered that my new wife had quit her job the week before our wedding. She was married now, she had no need for work. It was her job to look after me, have children and keep house. I accepted this as the norm and continued to worry about money. The Monday after the wedding I started up business as a Sole Trader doing Carpentry. We worked hard on the new business and made a living.

I am reminded of a funny thing that happened when I collecting the furniture I had purchased. I had a utility at the time and I went with Dad to collect it. The load was a bit too much for the ute to hold and Dad suggested we just put the big mattress on top of everything else that was already loaded on the back. I wanted to make another trip but Dad said it'll be right, he suggested he sit on top of it to hold it down. It was only a few kilometres home. So that's what we did. Well we came up the main street of town, Dad on the back hanging on to the mattress as best he could and the side of the ute. He was bouncing around a lot so I was going really slow. Not slow enough it turned out, as I went over a bump Dad, and mattress ended up on the bitumen. Dad on the bottom. Mattress on top. He had a few choice words to say about my driving abilities and I couldn't deny it because I couldn't open my mouth I was laughing to hard.

A couple of years into my first marriage we moved again as one of the companies I had apprenticed with asked me to return and run one of their businesses for them. They offered more than we were making so we went. 12 months later, we found ourselves with a baby coming along. My wife felt she needed to come home to her Mum. I always tried my best to do things that suited us both and I was a little overawed at the thought of a baby so I was glad to have her Mum close at hand. So we went back home and I started my own business once again. I was eventually the proud Dad of two children, the first a son and later a daughter.

My new business was a successful one and was to last around 20 years and provided us with a good life. Unfortunately, our marriage started to fade around 10years in, it had never been founded on true love, if there is such a thing. I'm pretty confused about the concept of True love. I thought I was in love a few times but it never lasted. Did I mess these up with too much expectation or assumption, could I have tried harder? Did I simply get bored? Unanswerable questions. Best left out.

We stayed together for a while. I did not want to leave until the kids had left home and she did not want me to leave at all so she was happy to accept that arrangement. We were not carrying on a physical relationship for many years and I took my interests elsewhere. She acted as if she never knew. Well I did tell her about some of this. If I thought it to be necessary. And I did a few times think it was necessary.

Why didn't I just leave? I wanted to be there with the kids. I didn't want to be my own Dad and if I left I knew I would feel like I was him. Dad never physically left my Mum but in many ways he was never really there at all. I stayed. Truthfully there was another reason I stayed. I loved her little Yorkshire terrier and couldn't see it left without me to look after it. When the little dog died of natural causes I finally left the house and went my own way. I don't think she believed I was actually going to leave but it was time, she was pretty mad so I went online and found her a boyfriend. He was married, and a bit of a lose unit but I wasn't to know that. It didn't work out I discovered. I also gave her the family home which was quite beautiful and overlooking the sea, and I bought her a new dog. What more can a man do. She stills hates me and is still mad at me. 20 something years later. At our daughter's wedding, on seeing me she proceeded to yell at me, like she had waited all those years to finish the lecture. After all that time you would think she would have calmed down just a little, apparently she hadn't.

In a random thought about children I received a letter from a former lover, a woman I had known in my younger years and later when we were a bit older. She was not known for her morals and I liked my women so not a long stretch to find us together on occasions. In this letter she told me I had a son, he was some 20 years old. She asked that I not contact him and that was that. She just wanted me to know. I am not sure if he is mine, no tests were done, so no proof but the fact she told me with no strings attached and wanting nothing of me somehow tells me he is. For a while he had lived up the road from us and once years before, my children had commented there was a boy at school who looked exactly like me. Strange world. I am not sure of her motives for telling me at this time but I had a daughter a few years younger. Perhaps she was just making sure I knew in case.

In the first year of my first marriage we were living in the small coastal town of Esperance some 450 kilometers from home. My wife had never really had my full attention and I liked my bit on the side. Am I proud of this, well actually I am. She was happy, I was happy and she never found out, so I think it was okay. The connection with one of my older female companions led to my embarking on a strange path. It did not interfere with my job as it was night work. My wife was totally unaware of my extra curriculum activities. How I pulled this off I have no idea.

I had been enjoying the favours of an older woman for a few weeks. She lived in a lovely apartment down on the waterfront and the fact that I even got in the door amazed me. Must have been able to see my prowess simply gleaming out of my eyes. I do have twinkling eyes; it has been commented on many a time. And the ladies did favour me. So I was a little taken back and somewhat annoyed when she offered me a night job. She asked me if I would like to earn some extra dollars and I was always struggling at this early stage, so I said of course I do. The job description came as a bit of a surprise, I was to escort women who found themselves alone in the city.

This job was strictly escorting she told me and I would get paid a percentage of the fee she charged and which she organized with the client. My wife and I were always struggling financially and we never had enough money. I tell myself this was my driving force. It would not be hard work I guessed. In truth sometimes it was. My meal was paid for and a night out to some nice places. I loved women so why not. Unfortunately, or fortunately depending on the woman, most of the women felt servicing their sexual needs was part of the job. Many were annoyed or angry when I had decided that if I went there it would cost an extra $100.00 and this went into my pocket. I was a male prostitute. I was a gigolo, if only I knew that word at the time. Sounds better than the first. But I was desperately poor, I had a wife to support, a mortgage and I was performing a service. Surely I can be forgiven this. All of them paid when it came down to it and no one complained about not getting their money's worth.

I was always attentive to their needs and not my own. I made sure they orgasmed at least once but more if I could and they were keen to keep going. I trained my mind, or that's what I think was happening, to not focus on myself and often would not come at all in the process. If I did ejaculate I was good to keep going for ages after so they were all well serviced. I hated the use of condoms, lost all feeling so I guess this helped me to slow down a bit. It feels like taking a shower in your overcoat or something like that. It takes away the delicious feeling of skin on slippery skin. I have rarely used them and up to this point not at all. I usually was in too much of a hurry to get one on. It was obviously necessary and the women would have insisted on it anyway. My boss was a bit serious about this as well.

I am not sure whether this portion of my working life is something to feel good about. What's done is done. Sometimes thinking back to this time fills me with humiliation but other times I tell myself it was justifiable under my circumstances. I was extremely poor, constantly under the stress of paying my way and my families way in life. This was not the most difficult way to make good money and the women were safe with me and got what they needed and wanted as well, so yes I'm okay with it. Sometimes!

One wedding story leads to another and this second wedding was a little more fun, though in my heart of hearts I knew this marriage was a decision that I was going to regret. I had been trying for a few months to disengage myself from this woman as our relationship was getting messed with by her kids. She would agree to part then turn up hysterical and crying that she loved me and couldn't cope without me. She vowed to sort her children and I do think she really thought she loved me but I think she loved my stability and my money more. I was too good a prize to lose. Well I think I was. Anyway I was to get married again. We got married on the beach I drove down on my motorbike with her in the side car. A thing she hated but I insisted. Hamish my dog was the bridesmaid and my son was the grooms man. She wore some weird medieval costume, probable a sign of the witch to emerge, and I wore leathers. She rode in the side car all the way to Fremantle with me and we had our reception at the yacht club, a rise in life from the Buffalo's hall those years ago.

Her children were the foulest mouthed evil children and they hated me yet they came to live with us. In my house. I soon learned that which I later told her. The piglets learn from the sow. I think you can see from this that our marriage soured pretty fast. Although we were to hang on for 10 years it was over about 3 years after we made that bike ride.

My years with this wife were pretty bad to say the least. She was a real bitch and did all she could to humiliate me especially when she couldn't get her own way or she was showing off to her friends. At a BBQ one night, which she was holding for her girlfriends, I offered to cook for them, and as usual when she drank too much the crap started. she began one of her favourite jokes about the girls not wanting to bother about me because of the size of my dick. I have a decent sized dick and I had asked her before not to use this particular taunt but she did it anyway. I was cooking for her friends and at this point a normal person may have got mad and walked away but I was truly pissed off and I have often been described as a little crazy, so I quite simple stepped out of my pants and undies and stood there cooking with all bits free to the air. She was furious. I had embarrassed her. I said that she should have listened to me. Maybe she would in the future. Now everyone knew what she was keeping to herself.

Once on one such party she had told me my company was not expected as it was a family 'do'. I didn't say anything but on the night I went along. She couldn't do much in front of everyone so we all had dinner. Everyone expected to pay their own meal, that's how they always did it. At the end of the meal, it was her birthday, I stood up and said 'The treat is on us tonight.' They were all thrilled but I hadn't brought my wallet. She was livid. I got my own back here and there. This was most satisfactory despite the anger; she was angry most of the time anyway. Money was always what motivated her and I had some money, especially when we met. I didn't leave with much of it. She saw to that one way or another.

If it were even possible to do so her children treated me worse and I was often ostracized in my own home. They would have family parties and they would say things like, it would be better if you went away for Christmas my family doesn't like you. In efforts to lessen the hostilities or simple because it was her birthday I would bring her a gift which she would take without even looking at me and I would see unwrapped weeks later. I knew I was not a part of her life anymore so decided it was time to go. We had a lovely home which I had built for us and I really enjoyed it.

I had bought a lovely home and renovated it. Once I painted the whole house over a few days. It was an old fashioned seventies yellow and I did it in a very beautiful, trendy mauve shade. She never noticed this. Eventually after a week of waiting I asked her if she liked it she said, 'oh that's what you've been doing.' Could not please her.

Our separation, when it came a few years later, was bitter. She cleaned me out and then to top it all off she wanted one of the dogs. I had bought my two Scottie's a few years before and they were my real loves. I refused to budge on this one point. The dogs were mine. I wasn't separating them and definitely wasn't leaving one with her. She told me she was keeping the dog and I told her I hope you can out run a bullet cos I'm coming back for the dog and you had better hand her over. Of course she couldn't miss this opportunity to hurt me more and the police landed on the doorstep demanding my guns. I had to surrender them. I still can't get them back. I was so livid I couldn't even look at her for fear of tearing her apart with my hands so I talked to my lawyer and said get my dog for me and left it to him to sort out. Of course she had me over a barrel and she put the screws in. If I want my own dog, then, for an additional $30000.00, she agreed I could have her. I paid the money and the dogs were reunited. I couldn't believe the twisted mind of someone who at some point had professed to love me. On one occasion she did tell me, 'I really did love you. I still do,' I said well I hate you and you'll never see the dogs or me again. She, who had just forced me to pay her an extra thirty thousand dollars in compensation to recover my own dog, said, 'you can be so cruel.' You can see why I don't like people too much and why I don't trust them. The times I have been badly hurt in this life have always involved people.

It was to be another 6 years before our divorce was settled and finally I'm free of the witch. During the divorce proceeding it seemed like the curse continued, on one occasion the judge would not look at the case as papers had been stapled instead of paper clipped. Bureaucracy gone mad. I try not to think of her or her monster offspring. I gave everything to these kids and one year they wrapped a bar of Cadbury's chocolate for me for Christmas. After my divorce and subsequent break down my sister told me. 'if I think you are looking like getting married again I'll cut your dick off.' I won't get married again. I like my dick.

Some people say to me why would you pay so much for a dog but to me they are very much a part of my life. They are friends and companions, not to be bartered for or used as weapons to hurt someone which was what she was doing. It suited her personality to be a bitch.

I have always loved dogs and had a deep empathy with them, all innocents really, I guess. My love probably started with the farm dogs. One incident that is still etched in my memory happened when I was a little kid. I would always try to befriend the working dogs. This was frowned upon but I did it anyway. When the dogs became unfit or too old to work Dad would tie them up and then shoot them. This was heartbreaking for me and the dogs seemed to know what was happening. One of these dogs, Lassie was his name, we had had for several years and he was a hard worker, he had finished working for the day and when we got home Dad went and got his rifle. Lassie went scooting fearfully under the shearing shed to hide when he saw Dad with the rifle in his hand. Dad crawled under the shed and shot him. He dragged him out and tossed him on the ute, like he was nothing. Like he had not worked for us all of his life. That was that. I vowed when I got my own dog I would treasure him for as long as he lived. My hatred for Dad burned stronger that day.

When I lived in that shed and I was doing my apprenticeship I really wanted a dog. I was lonely and I was cold. A dog would sort all of that out. One day I saw a sign near the workshop that read, Labrador puppies, $20.00. More than a week's wages but I scraped it together and off I went to get one. The night I brought him home he cried all night, missing his brothers and sisters, I guess, and he was vomiting up the food I had given him. All I had to give him was table scraps and they weren't that fancy. I decided about 4am, when neither of us had had any sleep, that at first light I would have to take him back. I crept up to the back fence and gentle dropped him over. I didn't ask for my money back just glad he was back with his family. I cleaned the shed and went to work. Poorer, still lonely and now hungry as well but happy with my decision.

Later I got my first Scottish terrier. Hamish. Hamish was not really a dog he was my best mate. At this time, I had a motor bike with a side car and he was my constant companion. He had his helmet, leathers and goggles and loved going for a ride. Losing Hamish to old age was like losing myself. I still miss him and some 15 years later I still grieve his parting. He was the best mate I ever had.

Life goes on

I say no to a week in Bali with a friend. I'm happy here in my own little world I say. As I say this I ponder the words. Am I happy? I feel safe here in this environment I have created. I don't need a lot and its peaceful, away from people.

I see people when I feel like it. I'm not sure about people. They are hard work sometimes. Who do you trust? Who do you embrace? I struggle sometimes to be bothered. I've got my dogs. But I do like to have company sometimes so maybe I care more than I'll admit even to myself. Especially female company. Still got all that working. Can't complain. Still love the chase.

Talking of Bali: I've had a few trips there, sometimes with company, wife's, friends, and sometimes alone. I'm laughing as I remember one trip. I arrived late in the day to my villa and as I was pretty tired from work I had a nap out by the pool in the sun, fully dressed in my clothes from Perth. I just sat down for a minute and I heard loud knocking. I jumped up. It was pitch dark. I had no idea where I was or what was happening. Searching for the source of the noise I stepped toward it. Straight into the pool. That certainly woke me up. Dripping wet, a bit annoyed I answered the door. I am amazed they served me again. What a surprise. Not just for me!

On one trip to Bali, travelling with one of my wives, second actually, not that it matters to the story, things got a little interesting. We both went to get something to read on the plane. She picked up a novel and I, not being a great reader, picked up the People magazine. I didn't open it on the trip. Nodding off instead. On arrival in Bali the staff became interested in my magazine and took it out of its plastic sealing. It had some women in various degrees of nudity. Not porn. Just boobs and bums sort of stuff. They wanted to confiscate the magazine and my wife, getting very mad at me, told me to just give it to them. No, I said there's no reason for them to have it and besides now I want to look at the women. After much discussion and shaking of heads, my wife's mainly, we were given the magazine and told we could leave.

One travel story leads the mind to another and I remember that during the years I was exploring photography I was taking pictures in the airport in Singapore while waiting for my flight. I was told not to take pictures of the guards but you know what that meant, red flag to a bull and of course I couldn't resist just one quick one. I was hauled away into an office and my camera taken and the film removed. I was questioned as to my identity and why I was taking picture.

I'm a photographer that's what I do. They questioned me for ages then let me go only to return and take me away again. Same thing over and over. Them getting excited and me getting upset. Eventually they let me go and I boarded the plane. While sitting on the air strip waiting to take off several armed guards boarded the flight. They walked up and down the aisle and I thought shit what now. Then they grabbed this man a few rows behind me and dragged him, kicking and screaming, off the plane. I was glad when we took off.

Internet Dating

Online dating. Now there's a thing.
Like fishing actually but this time you only have
yourself as bait. Not to go on too much about
internet dating but it is a bit of a quagmire out
there. Trying to get some sort of sense of who is who
and who is telling the truth and who is a scammer.
We used to call people like these con artists but now
they are called scammers. There's a lot of them.
Then there are people who are just crazy, desper-
ate, or down right horrible, liars, cheats, here and
there a few nice ones. Like me! In truth I've met a
few women that I am still friends with but usually it
doesn't go the way you plan. Or hope!

The innovation of the day. You put your name out there on a site, you write a few lines saying what a great romantic fellow you are, how much you love and respect women and you're there for the long haul. Then you post a picture off yourself. It's not easy to get a pic that makes you look great. Selfies are always difficult. I've learnt a few tricks to make you look your best. Smiling always attracts the ladies. When you're happy with the pic you sit back and wait for the masses of ladies to make contact. You get online and go through all the female profiles. You look at their pictures. You've long since learnt that no one actually looks like there picture, except you of course. It's like fishing really. I've always loved to fish. But I wonder how thick is my skin? I wonder if there is anyone out there for me. Am I up for a long term relationship.? What do I actually want? In truth I'm pretty flexible. Do I actually have enough time for a woman in my life? Do I really want one? Apart from my dogs I have no real ties. Of course there's the kids but they are grown up and happy, I have 3 grandkids as well. I will always see them but I don't live in their pockets. I'm not the loving, doting grandfather from story books.

In truth I like my own company and that of my dogs. I do however love the chase and like to bed a new woman. Somehow it makes me feel like I'm still in the game. There are a lot of women out there in the older set that are up for a romp in the bedroom. Lots have come out of boring marriages where their partner or husband simply can't get it up, or can't be bothered to do so. Some of the men are mean spirited bastards and the women are pretty much over them. I like to laugh, tell jokes. Make it fun. Mostly once I've done the bedding for a few weeks the relationship starts to become more routine, mundane, then eventually boring, then I'm ready to move on to the next challenge.

I've had some wonderful and some not so wonderful experiences. Some delightful and some really bizarre results from internet dating.

The most common story is women who put up pictures that are taken when Adam was a lad, or there abouts. They've aged, gone grey, gained weight. I'm no spring chicken but I do try to at least use a recent picture. I wonder what goes through someone's head when they do this. Do they think us men are too silly to notice? I'm not in the market for a very young woman and as I've pointed out I like my women as they come. Short, tall, plump, skinny. Love them all.

I have experienced women that simply want somewhere or someone to be with. One such woman, whom I had never met in the flesh, after discovering my address, showed up on my doorstep with her suitcases in hand and her car packed to the hilt. She was moving in! I felt that telling her where I lived was not so bad as she lived in Perth some five hundred miles to the north. A safe distance or so I thought. I was too soft to tell her to leave immediately so I gave her the bed and went and slept in my caravan. I locked my door. After a few days and my being very positive that she had to leave she reluctantly went on her way.

My heart has been broken more than once. Sometimes when things just don't work out and sometimes other things, like kids, get in the middle. At present Covid-19 is promising to destroy a blossoming relationship One that I felt was finally going in the right direction. I had met a lovely woman. An artist, from Sydney and after weeks of online chat and face timing we decided to meet up for real. She flew to Perth and I collected her at the airport. We spent a happy week in Perth then she came home to Albany with me. Several weeks of pleasant companionship, love and laughter she returned home to Sydney. We repeated this pattern of getting together as it was easier for her to travel. I had my dogs here in W.A. After her last trip I intended to travel to Sydney, meet her family and spend some time sightseeing together, we would spend a month there then come back together. Unfortunately, Covid-19 struck, the country was shutting down and borders were closing, we changed our plans and tried to get her back to WA but we were unable to do so. Weeks have turned to months and it has been so long now I'm not sure if it will ever be the same. I'm not sure now if I want to even date anyone. It is lonely here on my own. We aren't giving up and we won't stop trying but it is an exhausting and confusing system that lets some in and holds some out.

I've had a long history with online contacts, way back before it was, the 'in-thing', to be online. Before dedicated 'dating sites' there used to be a site called, ICQ. Read it out loud. You typed messages to each other and could contact anyone else on the site. It was very open and you could talk to anyone you wanted for however long and there were no fees no stamps, none of that stuff to make you part with your money. These days it's all about money and keeping you hooked and the scammers have a field day with us. Back then I was talking with a woman from the USA.

This was in the between days, those days between knowing my first marriage was over and leaving, It was one of the times I did tell my wife because after a year of chatting and telephoning and emails we decided to meet. I brought her out to Australia first and we had about 3months where we got on like a house on fire. Everything was good. She of course had to return home and I decided to go and visit her. This was an interesting and eye opening time for me. I enjoyed myself and even though I would have liked to find a way to stay with her I knew it was impossible, I had to go home and she, having three children, and an unsympathetic husband, could not leave them behind to come to Australia. I would not be able to work in the US either and she had very little money. The poverty of the area and the way she lived reminded me of the days when I was so poor I could barely eat, so I found myself helping her in all the ways I could.

One day, after she went go off to work, I was bored. so asked for her car keys and decided to take the old Cadillac, she drove, out for a spin. It was a huge car and I went to a shopping mall. It was snowing and the roads were slippery. I was trying to leave the car park but could not get traction on the slope and missed two sets of lights. The man driving a big ford truck behind me came up to my window and asked if I was leaving any time soon as he wanted to go home. I said, 'I'm trying to go but can't'. When the lights changed again I felt a jolt and I shot out onto the road with the Ford up my arse. That's the Americans, always finding unique ways to a problem. I had to go and tell her how the car got the big dent in the back but she didn't seem to mind and found the story amusing. I had the damage repaired.

I had some fun times in America and remember one incident when there was a dead skunk on the road and I, not knowing the consequence of making contact with a skunk, didn't bother avoiding it and I ran over it. She was shocked saying, 'you just ran over a skunk'! With a voice that said, is this man mad. I said It was already dead. She just looked at me and kept saying the same thing. 'You just ran over a skunk.' When we stopped the car and the awful smell reached us I knew what she was so upset about. Oh my goodness, what a smell. Despite several attempts to remove the smell, lots of hand washing and trips to the car wash, it took ages for the smell to dissipate, it probably never was completely gone. I became known locally known as the guy who ran over a skunk, and that was usually what people said to me when they met me, oh you're the guy who ran over a skunk. I always said 'It was dead!'

I would like to note here that I met my second wife on the internet. Not straight away but just another peril of the online dating thing. She turned out to be the date from hell.

I returned home to Australia and decided I need to do something different, a new start, so I bought an established business. With no fore knowledge of the retail industry I bought an Army surplus store. The day

I opened I was visited by the local bikie gang that proceeded to wreck the store as I did not have 'what they wanted'. Despite telling them it was my first day they were totally arrogant dickheads. There was too many of them for any other outcome than me being killed if I attempted to stop them, so I had to take it. I did not like that at all. I went to the previous owner and told him, 'a warning would have been nice', he said they were usually not too bad in fact he had been doing a fair bit of trade with them so he said he would talk to them. A few weeks later an envelope with two thousand dollars was placed on my counter 'for the damage'. After that a better working relationship was sorted.

If this incident was the start of trouble its solving certainly was not the end of it. There were some serious incidents at the store and eventually I closed the door and stored all of the stock at my warehouse in town. I was planning to sell it but after a number of years laying around gathering dust, mice shit and other crap was sent to landfill.

One such incident involved three Aboriginal men in their late teens coming into the shop wielding iron bars and looking for a fight. When I saw them entering I knew straight away I was in trouble. I rang my girlfriend quickly as I knew she was planning on coming into the store that day and told her to stay away. When I hung up I scanned for some weapon to help myself but nothing was available to me so I just prepared for a fist fight. I didn't do or say anything just waiting to see what was going to happen when one of the teenagers raised the bar to strike Hamish my little Scottie dog. Hamish had walked to greet them as he usually greeted all of my customers.

Without hesitation I jumped the counter and punched him hard in his face as he went to strike Hamish, the second man joined the fray and fists were flying fast. A woman who had a shop next door rushed in and, tiny as she was, jumped on the back of one of the men, the third man was not joining the fight and was trying to get the other two out of the shop. At this stage there were three fully grown men outside the store watching what was going on who did not come in even with the woman in the fight. I can only assume they had called the police and the aboriginals eventually ran off.

The police caught them a few hundred metres down the road and returned with them in tow to the shop. The Copper said, 'seeing they were holding you up we will take a statement from you and charge them'. The men were saying they had not held us up and I collaborated their words. I few seconds later they told me the man I had hit first had a broken jaw and if I pressed charges for the attack on my dog and me they would also press charges for excessive force. 'What'! I really had just about had it and thought what's the point in even trying. But a tiny part of me was thrilled and pretty happy that the teen had a broken jaw so I agreed not charge them. In my urgent haste to get across the counter I had broken the glass on the top of it so the incident did cost me money but me and Hamish were in one piece and it had been a good fight. The courageous lady from next door also came out unscathed. What a woman. Just goes to show how many sides a woman has. Another reason to love them all.

A week or so later a man came in to buy a jacket but he didn't have enough money. He asked for the closing time and said he would be back tomorrow. true to his word he was back at closing time the next day, I collected the jacket that I had on hold for him and brought it to the counter he came to the counter and paid for the jacket, as I opened the till to put the money in he produced a knife and said, 'I'll take my money back and yours as well'. This time around luck was on my side and a weapon did come to hand. A machete had been returned that day and I had set it just below the counter to deal with later. I could just reach the handle without moving too much so I grabbed it and pointed it at the guy who was wielding a six-inch blade. My blade was much bigger than his and his brave face faded to fear as he turned and ran. My Crocodile Dundee moment, and it felt good. I had a win that day as I got his money and kept my jacket and my life.

After surviving two ram raids I closed the door.

I decided to return to my cabinet making beginnings and I opened a new company I chose to specialize in building kitchens for the housing industry which was booming at this point and work was easy to come by. Too easy really and we grew rapidly, forcing me to employ staff and take on apprentices. These all required managing and some of them were pretty wild. A lot had the attitude of 'you need me' so I'll do as I like. These didn't last long. In the end I decided to cut back on contracts and workload and just kept two of my best, most reliable staff. This worked really well for a few years, but one of my best apprentices was to be the one that brought the business to its knees and me with it. He was a surfer and loved his wind surfing. He suffered a serious injury while out surfing. This of course was not covered by worker's compensation and off he went to Centre Link. It turned out that I owed him around $40,000.00 in unpaid leave and sick pay. Finding this large amount of money and losing him was a blow I found hard to deal with. So even though I had built a very successful business in the end it was just too hard. Once again I had reached the point where the business was no longer offering any enjoyment and I'd had enough, I'd done all I could and I was burnt out and just plain tired. I finished the contracts I had started then closed the doors and walked away.

Motor Bikes

I did love my bikes but when Hamish died I just couldn't do it anymore. I loved that dog. He was so much more than a companion; he was my mate. I would take him out for rides in the sidecar. He had his little helmet and goggles and was very amusing. Everyone loved him. Me especially!

I don't have a motor bike anymore, I used to really love them but now I just have a quad. I take out to go fishing and give the dogs a joy ride. It's harder now to use it on the beaches. So many rules and regulations. I feel sorry for kids especially. Maybe I'll get another bike one day. Better hurry up if I'm going to do it though. I'd have to get a double sidecar or something as I have two dogs now. Can't leave 'em home.

When I was around 17 I had an old motorbike given to me, it had many things wrong with it and I was pushing it home to work on it to see if I could get it going. On the way home I went passed, my now married, brother's house and he grabbed the bike off me, shoving me aside in his usual bullying way, and said I'll roll start it for you. I said, 'no don't as there's too many things wrong with it, I'm just going to push it home. 'He ran down the street got it started, jumped on and took off revving and sputtering down the road. Of course he burnt the motor out, completely, and there was no hope of fixing it now. I walked home and got the rifle, Mum was shouting at me to stop but I just kept going. I was off to my brothers, vengeance in mind. When I got there I headed straight out into the paddock, then Dad showed up, 'you can't shoot your brother mate', he's yelling. The fact he had got to me so fast and in such a panic tells me he knew I was capable of it. When he finally got hold of me I said 'I'm not shooting him I'm shooting his horse.' Even though Dad could appreciate the logic and black humour in this he talked me out of it and he said he would sort out my brother. My dickhead brother never changed he was a prick then and up till he died actually, even annoying me after his death. Cos the bastard left me as executor of his estate and it took me two years to get his estate settled as there was property to sell and get ready to sell. I did all that without any assistance from my lazy nephews, his lazy, good for nothing kids. He knew they were not capable of settling the estate. Now after it is all completed and the cash is in their pockets they don't want to pay me the $2000.00 claim made for the work and time. Little shits. It was actually the lawyer's idea that I claim this money, and he says it was worth a lot more. I was the good guy and said, 'No that will do.' What's the point in trying to do the right thing, to be reasonable?

Doesn't get you anywhere. Anyway we were talking about my bikes.

My first bike real bike was an old Enfield 125. It was painted in camouflage and the lights were blacked out. It was an old war bike, I scraped off the old paintwork and spruced it up and eventually I sold it for a profit which I used to buy a bigger, better bike. Looking back over the years and what they are worth now I should have garaged it for a few years. Money was always the driving force behind decisions. The new bike needed work and my Dad, a keen bike rider, helped me to do it up. Dad actually hated me riding so he was happy when I sold this bike as well. As a little kid I remember Dad riding home on a huge bike making a lot of noise and looking really cool.

I didn't get a new bike until after I was married the first time, My wife's cousins were bikers and they encouraged me to get a bike. I had started smoking so I justified this purchase by giving up smoking to make the monthly payments. We started a gang, but it wasn't a real gang back then. Our main activity was fighting, or street brawling really, usually with the local Aborigines and when that got boring the local surfers became the target.

We were a rather pathetic bikie gang by todays standard. We did not do drugs, we never raped anyone and the only things I ever remember being stolen were some drums of fuel and a five-gallon keg. The keg was thrown into the back of my brother's mini with about 4 guys squashed in with it. I was not in the stealing part of the days events but was definitely involved in the after party. We soon realised that without a spear to pierce the keg we could not open it. After much moaning and groaning and talking and finger pointing I suggested we buy a one. When I attempted to do so the cops were onto me straight away. Why would you want a spear, cos I'm going to buy a keg from somewhere else? They suggested I had stolen a keg from down the road but I could honestly say I did not. I came out of the pub spear less and we had to actually go and buy another keg with a spear.

We had spent all of our money to get this keg so we decided to have a party in a bush block near town and charge the guys $10.00 to come in, promising beer and girls. Of course when the cops arrived and asked where we would get the beer, we could honestly say we had bought a keg. How many people will be coming along, they asked, about 100 I said. they looked at me, laughed, and left us to it.

The cops were okay back in the day, they knew me from boxing and even though I was an enormous pain in the arse to them I was in truth pretty harmless. I was more danger to myself than anyone else.

One night the boys in the gang broke into a depot to steal fuel, they got about 4 drums but when they got home it turned out to be kerosene. One of the guys worked out how to run the mini on kerosene - we simple had to start it with petrol then switch to kerosene. How he worked this all out is beyond me but I was usually pretty easily persuaded to give something a go.

This mate also taught me how to jump start a car without a key. I was pretty happy with this new found skill and anxious to show it off. One day I found a person in need of such skills outside his home on the roadside. He had his head under bonnet doing his bit and I was sitting in front doing mine. Unfortunately, I had the car in gear and as it started it lurched forward knocking him over and under the car. I took off before he got up. The yelling and swearing coming from under the car told me he wasn't hurt but I wasn't waiting around.

Reflection

*I feel in a way I have always been two people. There
was one of me that was kind and gentle and loving
and the other was always looking for adventure and
excitement was always ready to go to extremes to
feel and this person scared me sometimes.*

W ell what would I change if I had my life over.
There's not much I regret. A few fights. A few
women I should have said no to. But not much.

I feel in a way I have always been two people. There
was one of me that was kind and gentle and loving
and the other was always looking for adventure and
excitement and this person scared me sometimes. I
knew to what lengths I would go. Even now he raises
his head and whispers in my ear. The one that arches
up when he feels threatened or questioned. Having
said this since that fight in my fifties I would do anything not to fight, I would run a mile, hide, whatever it
took to not get involved. Although I place little score
by the star signs I realize I am a fine example of mine.
I am a Gemini and the twin aspect of this sign is definitely me.

I had been taught from a young age that softness

was weakness. I tried to live that way but I was not uncaring and hard. I cared for others but I also wanted to please. Sometimes pleasing Mum and Dad was being hard and tough. Doing the stuff that the others wouldn't. Sometimes it was shutting up and keeping things to yourself when they should have been able to be told. Some of my secrets have not been revealed even to myself in this reflection on my life. I can't share them I can't even think about it; it is too painful.

The loving caring part of me tried to protect the ones I loved from the other part. I didn't always make this happen and often they would suffer the consequences of my dual personalities and antics, even though they were unaware of this. If I felt that the part of me I didn't want to show was in danger of being revealed I disengaged from the relationship or situation. I often did this without explanation leaving confused people in my wake. Being in love is to me a loss of control, not of the person but of myself, I don't like this feeling.

I think my Dad saw the wild side of me and he used it to his advantage. I was the family enforcer and he would send me to give people the 'stand down' order, if they didn't and persisted in whatever it was that they were doing I gave them a belting. Most did back down my reputation was enough to deter anyone from getting into a fight with me.

I often didn't think things through and as a young person this got everyone in trouble and quite often me. One night a young woman asked if she could go to a party in town with me. I said I'm going and I can give you a lift but I'm not taking you as a date or any such thing. She was okay with this. When we arrived I went off drinking with the other guys and she mingled. The party was mostly male so she was being given lots of attention. She was soon led off to a bedroom with one of the guys and I noted this but it was not my business and no one forced her in there. A while later I noticed one of the others going into the room and so I took more notice and when he left a third young man entered the room. This was not good, and the part of me that did not want anyone harmed came to the front. I made sure I was next in line and went in. I said, 'are you alright?' and she said, 'How many more because I've had enough.' I knew she would not get out of this easily because the boasting had started outside and lots of drunken males were eager to prove themselves. I said to her 'get dressed quick and get out of the window and run'. She did and I stayed in the room for about thirty minutes. Soon they bashed in the door to see what I was doing in there all that time. When they discovered I had allowed her the time and shown her how to get out they beat me up. I took a few of them out but the weight of numbers was against me and I could not win. I was black and blue but I still felt like I had done what was right. I never took any one to a party again unless she was mine and under my protection. She was there for sex and she got what she wanted but it was getting out of hand. The two parts of me fought that night. If

I had turned a blind eye and decided she knew what she was doing I would have had regrets for the rest of my life. Even know I wish she had not convinced me to take her to that house.

I fed the adventurous part of my life with the motorcycles, the fights with the surfies, and picking fights where and when I felt the need. I loved the adrenalin of it while at the same time I was a master craftsman, winning awards and having a reputation as an expert in my field. My work was perfect and I was fair and considerate in my dealings with my clients. The scent of the wood, the smoothness of its surfaces and the beauty of a well-made piece of furniture calmed me and gave me a different type of pleasure.

The boxing in my life also kept my wilder side under control. I could take out all frustrations in th9/e ring. I often went into a fight full of focus and energy, intent on the victory and after the fight felt extremely sad and full of regret.

It sometimes worked in reverse. During the lead up to my second marriage. I was fully aware I should walk away and leave this woman. When I did manage to get through to her we were over she would come to me crying and begging me to forgive her, that she had it all sorted out and I would feel sorry for her and give in. This was to result in the terrible marriage I suffered my way though. My soft, caring side would get its way and that too led to problems. I often felt trapped by these contrary forces that were a part of me.

When I finally left my second marriage, I bought

a van and thought I might travel a while around the country, I went to my daughter's farm in Albany for a few days but I was in such a state I decided to stay there a while. I remember when I arrived I was a broken man. I walked in the trees and sat and wept like a child. I was drained, exhausted and emotionally devastated. She and her children had spent years breaking me down. I felt defeated and like I was nothing. She constantly and systematically belittled me until I began to think she was right I lost sight of myself. It took a while but with the countryside around me, the solitude and my two constant companions, my little Scotties, I slowly got better and the side of me that always fights found his way through the dark tunnel to the light of day. A new start and a chance for a new adventure. Who knew what possibilities the future held. The side of me that loves life and refuses to give in had won the day.

So in conclusion I sometimes feel I never knew what side of me was right and which side to listen to, mostly I never thought about it, just went with my gut. Do I have regrets? Yes, some, but in truth I am what I am and everything that has happened to me, the good and the bad, have fashioned me for this last period of my life. I could have made different choices along the way but I am not sure looking back what they would have been. I could have saved myself some pain but then there is a lot of material for laughing at these days. I am happy, I keep trying, the base I've established for myself here on the farm gives me pleasure and a security for the future. I've met a lady I feel like might finally be the one....

Dawn La Puma - Author

Dawn was born in Geraldton, WA, and has lived in most areas of Australia, in both big cities and tiny country towns, such as Sandstone in WA's goldfields and also in the Pilbara. Dawn has also lived in the USA and visited Europe and Asia New Zealand and the South Pacific. She now lives in the Great Southern region in the delightful little town of Denmark, W. A. Here she owns and runs a Gallery, Café and Bookshop.

She is a mother and a grandmother of five. Dawn loves to dance and loves music. She is currently learning to play the Djembe drums. Life is for living.

Dawn has always loved stories both reading and writing them. Her favourite genre is fantasy but here and there a story that should be told just sorts of pops up into your life.

Her philosophy for life is very simple and uncomplicated. She endeavors to embrace life, each and every day, to honor the spiritual aspects of life and to love and uphold her family and friends.